THREE
HUGE
NOVELS

* Not all of these titles are available at the time of publication.

3 Huge Novels

Vicente Huidobro & Hans Arp

translated from Spanish by
Tony Frazer

Shearsman Books

First published in the United Kingdom in 2020 by
Shearsman Books Ltd
PO Box 4239
Swindon
SN3 9FN

Shearsman Books Ltd Registered Office
30–31 St. James Place, Mangotsfield, Bristol BS16 9JB
(this address not for correspondence)

ISBN 978-1-84861-724-7

First published with these contents, in Spanish, as *Tres inmensas novelas*
by Ediciones Zig Zag, Santiago, 1934.
A French translation of the first three stories, by Rilka Walter,
appeared in Paris in 1946 under the title *Trois nouvelles exemplaires*.

ACKNOWLEDGEMENTS
We are grateful to the Stiftung Arp, e.V., Remagen and Berlin,
for permission to publish the three jointly-authored stories in this volume.

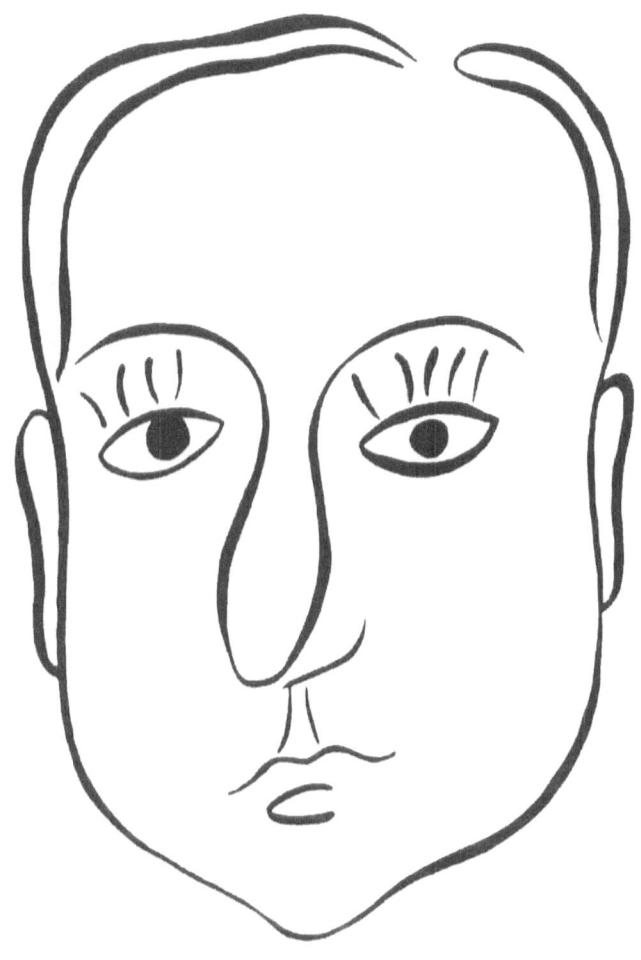

Vicente Huidobro, by Hans Arp

Hans Arp, by Amadeo Modigliani

CONTENTS

INTRODUCTION

The first three stories in this volume – the *Tres novelas ejemplares* – were written in French by Huidobro and Arp while on holiday with their families in Arcachon (in the Gironde, south of Bordeaux) in 1931, French being the only language the two had in common. There is very little information in the public domain about the original manuscript of the book but it must have been lost before the end of World War II. The stories remained unpublished until 1935, when Huidobro placed his Spanish translation of the originals (together with two additional stories of his own, the book otherwise not being long enough) with ZigZag, a Santiago publisher. Those translations appear to date from 1932, judging by the letter to Arp included here as a prelude to the second half of the book. The original book – that is, the jointly-authored stories only – finally appeared in France in 1946 with the Parisian publisher, Fontaine, in their 'Collection "L'age d'or" dirigée par Henri Parisot', a series devoted to surrealist books, in a re-translation from Huidobro's Spanish text by Rilka Walter, as the original text was by then no longer extant.

Thus, we present our translation here of, and together with, the 1935 Spanish text, although the latter *has* also been compared to later reprintings, in the 1966 *Obras completas*, and the 2007 edition of the two-handed stories by Abada Editores, Madrid. There appear to be two previous translations into English, one from the French by Joachim Neugroschel (in *Arp on Arp*; Viking, Documents of 20th Century Art, 1972; 2nd edition, as *Collected French Writings*, MIT Press, 1980), and one from the Spanish by Tom Raworth. However, this latter version – which covered all five stories, unlike the Neugroschel translation – appeared only in a very limited edition issued by Face Press in 2017, under the title *Save Your Eyes*, where the author is listed as Raworth rather than Huidobro / Arp, even though the book's blurb clearly states that it is a translation. To add one further wrinkle to the story, in 2005 or thereabouts, Tom Raworth and I discussed the possibility of including at least some of that translation – although at that stage, he did not possess a copy of it – in a book to be published here. The Huidobro volume that I then envisaged did not come together, however, until 2019 – and by then it had turned into a large *Selected Poems*, with two manifestos thrown in

for good measure; not, then, a book that could easily have encompassed these stories as well.

The original title of the work, and here the title of the first section, which contains the jointly-authored stories, was *Tres novelas ejemplares* [Three Exemplary Novels], which one must assume to be a playful reference to Cervantes (*Novelas ejemplares*, published 1613) and perhaps also to Miguel de Unamuno's *Tres novelas ejemplares y un prólogo* (1920), the title of which was certainly a deliberate echo of Cervantes. The Unamuno was available in French translation by 1925, and thus could possibly have been known to Arp also. The fact that the stories themselves show no trace of influence from Cervantes or Unamuno is presumably part of the joke. One should also clarify that *novela* means both "novel" and "novella" in Spanish, although the latter is more often referred to as "novela corta" (short novel). The title of the 1946 French edition has it as "novellas", because the French word *nouvelles* is used, rather than *romans*.

Ejemplar, as an adjective, means "exemplary", and that is how the Cervantes title is always translated. Huidobro plays with the word in his solo contribution to the book, titling his pair of stories collectively as *Dos ejemplares de novela*, using the fact that the noun, *el ejemplar*, means "specimen", or a "copy" (as in "a copy of a book"). I have translated it as "example" here, which is slightly less accurate than some other possibilities, but which affords a useful echo of the first subtitle.

The stories themselves, and especially the jointly-authored ones, are almost textbook examples of Surrealism: whimsical stories with echoes of fairytales, and what looks at times like a kind of chain composition, where each author writes a line, or sentence (or part thereof) and hands the text back to his partner, who then does likewise. In any event, they are splendidly silly, and I hope that they will be of interest to anglophone readers. The text here follows the 1935 edition, albeit corrected in places where the original had obvious typographic errors or failed to get French accents right – the Chilean typesetters seem to have been confused by *grave* accents in particular. A few errant spellings have been left as such and are explained in the Glossary at the end of the volume. In perhaps a dozen cases I have departed from the strict sense of the original text, where I have tried to replicate, as well as I could, the wordplay in which Huidobro indulged.

Huidobro had arrived in Europe from Chile in late 1916 and promptly made a name for himself in vanguard circles in Paris, mixing with the leaders of the new movement in poetry (Apollinaire, Jacob, Reverdy, Tzara), befriending many of the following wave (Cocteau, Cendrars among the French, Gerardo Diego, Juan Larrea and others in Spain), mixing with the most forward-thinking artists (Picasso, Gris, Picabia, Arp, Delaunay, Lipchitz) and composers (above all, Edgard Varèse who set Huidobro's words to music). In a bewildering period of 24 months – the calendar years 1917–18 – he published two full collections, *Horizon carré* [Square Horizon; in French] and *Poemas árticos* [Arctic Poems; in Spanish], as well as four chapbooks, two in Spanish, and two in French.

In the aftermath of the war, Huidobro calmed down a little, although he remained busy writing, publishing poems in magazines, editing magazines, writing polemics and manifestos and turning his hand to prose and to screenplays for silent films. He published a short selected poems in French in 1921, *Saisons choisies* [Selected Seasons], and travelled throughout Europe giving readings and lectures.

1925 saw the publication of two books of poems in French, *Automne régulier* [Ordinary Autumn] and *Tout à coup* [All of a Sudden], along with a volume of manifestos (*Manifestes*), and a year later, when the author was back in his native Chile, there followed a volume of essays and aphorisms, *Vientos contrarios* [Adverse Winds]. The 1920s also saw the publication of two novels, one play, and an anti-British diatribe, *Finis Britanniae*; in 1931 Huidobro published the books I consider to be his masterpieces, *Altazor* and *Temblor de cielo* [Skyquake] in Madrid. Although he often railed against Surrealism in manifestos and essays, his work from 1925 onwards is indelibly marked by it, and Hans Arp, his partner in this volume, was very much part of the movement, as well as its forerunner, Dada.

Hans Arp was born in Strasbourg, Alsace, the son of a French mother and a German father, during the period following the Franco-Prussian War when Alsace was part of the German Empire, France having ceded it after defeat in 1871. Alsace returned to France in 1918 as part of the reparations after World War I, was again swallowed up by the Third Reich in 1940, and returned finally to France in 1945 after a public plebiscite. Arp referred to himself as Jean in France and Hans in German-speaking countries.

After leaving the École des Arts et Métiers [School of Arts and Crafts] in Strasbourg in 1904, he went to Paris where he published his first

poems. From 1905–1907, Arp studied at the Weimar Kunstschule [Art School] in Germany, and returned to Paris in 1908, where he attended the Académie Julian. Arp was a founder-member of the Moderne Bund [Modern Alliance] in Lucerne, participating in their exhibitions from 1911 to 1913. In 1912, he met Vasily Kandinsky in Munich, and exhibited with Kandinsky's influential Blaue Reiter [Blue Rider] group. Later that year, he took part in a major exhibition in Zurich, with Matisse, Delaunay and Kandinsky. In 1913, his work was taken up by Herwarth Walden, the Berlin dealer and magazine editor who at the time was one of the most significant arbiters of taste in the European avant-garde.

In order to escape from the war (and presumably also to avoid any complications caused by his double nationality) Arp moved to Switzerland in 1915. It transpired that Zurich was *the* place to be in 1915–16. Hugo Ball opened the Cabaret Voltaire in 1916, where the future Dada group came together: Arp, Richard Huelsenbeck, Hans Richter, Tristan Tzara, among others. In 1920, Arp set up the Cologne Dada group with Max Ernst and Alfred Grünwald. In 1925, his work also appeared in the first Surrealist exhibition at the Galerie Pierre in Paris, thus ensuring that Arp formed a bridge between the two groups. In 1926, Arp relocated to Meudon, near Paris. In 1931, he left the Surrealists to join the Paris-based constructivist group *Abstraction-Création* with their associated journal *transition*, edited by Eugène Jolas, and in which Huidobro also published. His work began to change around this time from collages and bas-reliefs to include bronze and stone sculptures, and he also produced several small works made from multiple elements that the viewer could rearrange into new configurations, thus ensuring that Dada chance operations continued to play a role in his work. For the rest of of his life he was regarded as a major figure in contemporary sculpture, his biomorphic forms exerting considerable influence on both sides of the Atlantic.

He wrote poetry and essays throughout his life, both in French and in German, much of which has been translated into English, although more so from French than from German.

Tony Frazer
June 2020

HANS ARP y
VICENTE HUIDOBRO

TRES
NOVELAS
EJEMPLARES

(Arcachón 1931)

HANS ARP and
VICENTE HUIDOBRO

THREE
EXEMPLARY
NOVELS

(Arcachon 1931)

SALVAD VUESTROS OJOS

(Novela posthistórica)

Era el día de Navidad, el 1º de mayo. Del cielo caían hombres de nieve y toneles llenos de truenos. Sobre el mundo flotaban los tres últimos corazones calafateados: la Libertad, la Igualdad, la Fraternidad. Era el último día del nuevo año. El árbol del idealismo, ese árbol sentimental en el cual se mecían los nidos de los filósofos materialistas, fue abatido de golpe por un solo trueno de helium.

Los hombres se habían convertido en cebollas cocidas, con un palillo de dientes entre los dedos de los pies y una bandera de colores sagrados en el ojal derecho del pantalón izquierdo. Diez minutos más tarde, los hombres habían desaparecido y la última mujer masticaba sus píldoras orientales, sentada sobre las teclas de la más alta montaña de la tierra. Tenía un cierto parecido con el Arca de Noé, aunque su barba era un poco más larga y su palomo un poco más corto.

Sin embargo, llevaba en el pico de su mirada aviesa una hermosa rama de olivo. (Este olivo se ha convertido hoy en el alfiler de corbata de los cortacircuitos especializados).

Como el lector debe haber comprendido, el hombre ha desaparecido de la faz de la tierra, y en su lugar, podemos ver al *glóbulo hermafrometálico*, esbelto, y elegante, no más ancho que la mitad de la oreja del Angelus de la tarde, ni más largo que el meridiano de Greenwich a las 6.40 del día.

Este ser, elegante y esbelto, está perfectamente standarizado y se puede comprar por dos francos cincuenta en todos los almacenes bien provistos. Su espacio individual no pasa le 25 centímetros cúbico. Cuando su respiración excede algo más allá de esta medida, él la pliega en dos y aun en tres, según las circunstancias.

Aquí debemos advertir, para la perfecta comprensión de nuestra historia, que estos seres, cuando se encuentran aislados, se llaman Antonio, y cuando se les encuentra en grupos, se llaman José. Sus mujeres, cuando la cantidad de glóbulos que las forman pasan de un metro de al tura, se llaman Carolina; cuando no llegan a un metro, se llaman Rose Marie.

Los Antonios, que desde hace tanto tiempo han sobrepasado nuestro plano físico de vanguardia colectiva y nos han aniquilado completamente,

SAVE YOUR EYES

(Posthistorical novel)

It was Christmas Day, the 1st of May. Snowmen and barrels full of thunder fell from the sky. Above the world floated the last three caulked hearts: Liberty, Equality, Fraternity. It was the last day of the new year. The tree of idealism – that sentimental tree in which the nests of materialist philosophers swayed – was suddenly struck down by a single clap of helium thunder.

Men had turned into boiled onions, with toothpicks between their toes and a flag of sacred colours in the right-hand button-hole of their left trouser leg. Ten minutes later, men had disappeared and the last woman was sitting on the peak of the highest mountain on earth, chewing her oriental pills. She had a certain resemblance to Noah's Ark, though her beard was a little longer and her cock pigeon a little shorter.

However, she bore at the summit of her perverse gaze a beautiful olive branch. (This olive has today become the preferred tie-pin of specialist circuit-breakers.)

As the reader must have realised, Man has disappeared from the face of the earth and instead what we can see is the *hermaphrometallic globule*, slender and elegant, no broader than half the ear of the evening Angelus, and no longer than the Greenwich meridian at 6:40 a.m.

This elegant and slender being is perfectly standardised and can be bought for two francs fifty in any well-stocked store. It takes up no more space than 25 cubic centimetres. When its breathing takes it beyond this measure, it folds into two, or even into three, depending on the circumstances.

Here we must make clear, so that our story might be perfectly understood, that these beings are called Antony when they are on their own, and they are called Joseph when found in groups. Their wives are called Caroline when the quantity of their formative globules exceeds one metre in height; if they fail to reach one metre, they are called Rosemary.

The Antonys – that for so long now have surpassed our cutting-edge collective physical plane and have completely annihilated us – the

los Antonios repito, llevan en el sitio en donde nosotros llevábamos los bigotes almidonados, magníficas corrientes alternativas que tienen el gesto altivo del índice que Virgilio dejó olvidado en un tronco de árbol, pocos días antes de su muerte. Esto en cuanto a los bigotes, ahora en cuanto a los otros pelos que a nosotros nos servían para saber la hora precisa en cualquier momento del día o de la noche, ellos no los poseen, pero tienen en su sitio pequeños arco iris cantantes, cubiertos cada uno de hemisferios de aluminio.

Los Josés tienen un carácter que se asemeja al paladium 36, que es más ligero que el agua y sus lebreles. Los Josés son transparentes como la estratósfera antes del descubrimiento de América. Van rodeados de un círculo de humo que les confiere un aire coqueto, gracioso e higiénico. Poseen un talento especial para descifrar los jeroglíficos del tiempo de los hombres. Ellos descifraron el magnífico himno religioso que aquí incluimos para solaz y meditación de nuestros cultos lectores:

Cuando vosotros hayáis empleado los anteojos eternos con perfume de meteoros para vuestra T^8 o vuestra M^{15}, vosotros no rascaréis jamás el infinito ni la tormenta de la élite del mundo elegante, ni el lagarto africano sobre todas las grandes marcas.

Buena suerte, el día de gloria ha llegado con el big Satán desnudo, sólo después de medianoche, cuyo renombre mundial de vías urinarias va creciendo siempre.

Cualquiera que sea vuestro nuevo cuadro de adherencias, no agravéis el mal rascándoos el marinero, pues el órgano excepcional os da absoluta seguridad.

Si tortugas voladoras obscurecen vuestra vista, si vuestra nariz aparece lacrimosa y pegada en las mañanas contra los muros y vuestros labios son rápidos, como los servicios de la muerte o las preparadoras y picadoras de tallos, no os asustéis. Ello significa siempre la esencia de las más altas temperaturas.

"*Allons enfants de la patrie*, salvad los ojos de los marineros."

Para la perfecta comprensión de nuestra historia, debemos ahora dar algunos detalles sobre las Carolinas y también sobre las Rose Maries. Las Carolinas son glóbulos hermafrometálicos con un talle permanente de películas protectoras sobre las piezas movibles. Cuando empiezan a girar están frías y dan un mejor funcionamiento. Su temperatura es considerable cuando la presión influye sobre sus cualidades lubricantes, pero las impurezas que se deslizan no perjudican a su dicacidad. Ellas absorben el calor, y es de suma importancia el vaciarlas a menudo.

Antonys, I repeat, wear in place of the waxed moustaches we used to wear, magnificent alternating currents that bear the haughty index-finger gesture that Virgil left behind in a tree trunk a few days before his death. So much for the whiskers; as for the other hairs which we employed to tell the exact time at any point of the day or night, they do not have them; in their place however they have little singing rainbows, each covered with an aluminium hemisphere.

The Josephs have a character that resembles Palladium 36, which is lighter than water and their greyhounds. The Josephs are transparent like the stratosphere before the discovery of America. They walk enveloped in rings of smoke which lends them a flirtatious, witty and hygienic air. They have a special talent for deciphering hieroglyphics from the Age of Man. They deciphered the magnificent religious hymn that we include here for the solace and meditation of our learned readers:

When you have used eternal eyeglasses with the scent of meteors for your T^8 or your M^{15}, you will never again scratch against the edge of infinity, nor the storm of the elegant world's elite, nor the African lizard on all the great labels.

Good luck, the day of glory has arrived with the great naked Satan, only after midnight, the fame of whose urinary tract just keeps on growing throughout the world.

Regardless of who sees your new adhesion chart, do not aggravate the evil by scratching the sailor, for this exceptional organ offers you complete safety.

If flying turtles obscure your view, if your nose appears tear-stained and stuck to the walls in the morning, and if your lips are quick as the services of death or those who prepare and grind stalks, do not be afraid. This always indicates the essence of the highest temperatures.

"*Allons enfants de la patrie*, save the sailors' eyes."

So that our story might be perfectly understood, we must now give some details concerning the Carolines, and the Rosemarys too. The Carolines are hermaphrometallic globules with a one-size-fits-all protective film covering their moving parts. When they start spinning they are cold and offer better performance. Their temperature is considerable when the pressure influences their lubricating qualities, but impurities that slip in do not harm their efficiency. They absorb heat, and it is crucial that they be emptied often.

Las Rose Maries son perversas. En su trayecto a través del mundo absorben y evacuan una gran cantidad de vitaminas celestes. Esta participación a la vida, sólo puede ser asegurada por un magnetismo de primera clase en venta en bidones sellados. Ello es una garantía para vuestra vida privada y económica.

Estos seres han transformado el mundo, han barrido los continentes y los mares de la tierra. La Australia se ha convertido en un ruido colectivo, Europa es un ojal para las legiones de nebulosas y las condecoraciones de danzas postparanóyicas. Del África hicieron un estercolero tricolor para la electricidad arcaica de los aeroplanos sentimentales o venecianos, perfumados de jazmín y los altoparlantes de la sabiduría.

Aquí debemos advertir, para la perfecta comprensión de nuestra historia, que los únicos seres que no pudieron ser barridos por los glóbulos hermafrometálicos fueron las ardillas. Estas pequeñas snobs de los pinos, estas comedoras de luto, estas fabricantes de motores a corazón, estas paladeadoras del dolor, estas decapitadoras de las hermanas de los incas, estas inventoras del viento norte, se paseaban sobre los desiertos del racionalismo, burlándose de los glóbulos hermafrometálicos. Les hacían sentir el aroma de lavanda e imitaban los gritos y los cantos de los búhos, de los relojes y de los curas, de tal modo que los glóbulos temblaban como nosotros ante los espectros. Servían salchichas descentradas y mostraban imágenes vergonzosas del tiempo de las revoluciones cuando los burgueses se empecinaban en defender y propagar su lepra ultravioleta. Entonces los glóbulos enrojecían y los coladores que las protegían contra toda metafísica empezaban a estornudar como cuentos de hada. ¿Quién podía garantizar a los glóbulos hermafrometálicos que las ardillas no poseían un poder cabalístico y que de un instante al otro no harían surgir praderas materialistas llenas de miosotis y de confesionarios? ¡Ah! Estas pequeñas vengadoras y revendedoras de la melancolía, estos sacerdotes del buen comer, eran enemigos encarnizados del Antonismo y del Josefismo, de la higiene y de las matemáticas.

¿Por qué razón hemos olvidado hablar de América y de Asia? Debía de haber alguna razón para semejante olvido. No había razón alguna para tal olvido. América se convirtió en un suspiro perforado. El Asia se convirtió en un fuego fatuo sutil y prestidigitador. Así, pues, los cinco continentes no ladraban más en las noches de luna.

Para la perfecta comprensión de nuestra historia, debemos contar al lector lo que sucedió una tarde del año $O^3 Z^7$.

The Rosemarys are perverse. In their passage through the world they absorb and evacuate a large quantity of celestial vitamins. This participation in life can only be assured by top-class magnetism which is sold in sealed barrels. This is a guarantee for your private life and your economic life too.

These beings have transformed the world: they have swept the continents and the seas from the earth. Australia has been turned into a collective noise; Europe is a buttonhole for legions of nebulae and the insignia of post-paranoiac dances. Out of Africa they made a tricoloured dunghill for the archaic electricity from sentimental or Venetian aeroplanes, scented with jasmine and loudspeakers of wisdom.

Here we should make clear, so that our story might be perfectly understood, that the only beings which could not be swept away by hermaphrometallic globules were squirrels. These little snobs from the pine-trees, these consumers of grief, these manufacturers of heart engines, these relishers of suffering, these decapitators of the Incas' sisters, these inventors of the North Wind, strolled across the deserts of rationalism, mocking the hermaphrometallic globules. They made them smell the aroma of lavender and imitated the cries and songs of owls, clocks and curates, so that the globules trembled as we do when we see apparitions. They served maladjusted sausages and displayed shameful images from the revolutionary era, when the bourgeois insisted on defending and propagating their ultraviolet leprosy. Then the globules blushed and the sieves that protected them against all metaphysics began to sneeze as if in a fairy tale. Who could guarantee the hermaphrometallic globules that the squirrels did not possess kabbalistic powers and that from one moment to the next they would not give rise to materialistic meadows filled with forget-me-nots and confessionals? Ah! These little avengers and retailers of melancholy, these priests of fine dining, were ferocious enemies of Antonyism and Josephism, of hygiene and mathematics.

Why have we neglected to mention America and Asia? There must have been some reason for such an omission. There was *no* reason at all for such an omission. America turned into a perforated sigh; Asia turned into a subtle and magical will 'o the wisp. That is why the five continents no longer barked on moonlit nights.

So that our story might be perfectly understood, we must relate to the reader what happened one afternoon in the year O^3Z^7.

Rose Marie se paseaba por las selvas flúidicas, contemplando en pequeños espejos de centellas sus hermosos labios indefrisables, cuando de repente encontró una vieja caverna olvidada. La curiosidad, esa virtud de los ascensores y de los timbres eléctricos, la hizo penetrar en sus laberintos. Después de mucho andar en las tinieblas, encontró tendido entre las rosas el cadáver petrificado de un viejo lobo del aire, con la pipa aún humeante entre los labios y el rostro quemado por los soles inocentes de la prehistoria filosófica.

Rose Marie sentía las atracciones generatrices y los imanes genitivos de José, y, como es natural, corrió a contarle su hallazgo. Todo el mundo sabe que los Josés, gracias a una larga experiencia, a sus instrumentos constantemente perfeccionados y a la excelencia de sus métodos, producen un calor capaz de satisfacer plenamente cualquier exigencia. Pero la experiencia que antes nacía sólo en la punta extrema de cada cabello blanco y que ahora nace tres meses antes que ellos empiecen a echar raíces, les ha enseñado a evitar los momentos peligrosos y salvar dignamente las dificultades por medio de un simple deslizamiento de dos piezas aisladoras, fa una contra la otra, lo que produce una protección eficaz y permanente de sus propiedades climatéricas íntimas y reduce a la nada todo los ataques. José, seguro de sí mismo, siguió a Rose Marie en medio de la selva flúidica y bajó con ella hasta el fondo de la caverna perdida. Allí, como podía preverse, la discusión estalló.

—Te afirmo que no es un viejo lobo del aire— dijo José—. Es el futuro soldado desconocido.

—Desengáñate— exclamó Rose Marie desdeñosa—, no cabe duda de que es un viejo lobo del aire; mira cómo la pipa humea entre sus labios y cómo sus manos tienen forma de aterrizaje forzoso.

—Yo no veo tal aterrizaje forzoso y en cuanto a la tal pipa, ella no es sino un cometa que le cuelga de la boca, o, si prefieres, una especie de vómito de fuego en el cual se ve una brújula que marca noventa años, después del nacimiento de José. Sostengo que es el futuro soldado desconocido; mira cómo le brotan medallas sobre la nariz y observa su sonrisa socarrona.

—Imposible. Si fuera el futuro soldado desconocido, daría evidentes signos de vida. Además, eso probaría que iban a haber aún guerras, lo cual es un grave error científico, como tú sabes.

—Nunca he dicho que sea el soldado desconocido de futuras guerras nuestras, no me tomes por imbécil, digo que iba a serlo de las guerras

Rosemary was strolling through the rainforests, contemplating her beautiful non-abrasive lips in little sparkling mirrors, when suddenly she found an old forgotten cave. Curiosity, that virtue of elevators and electric doorbells, moved her to enter into its labyrinths. After walking for some time in the darkness, she found stretched out amongst the roses the petrified corpse of an old air-wolf, a pipe still smoking between its lips, and its face burned by the innocent suns of philosophical prehistory.

Rosemary felt Joseph's generative attractions and his genitive magnets, and, as you would expect, ran to tell him of her discovery. Everyone knows that the Josephs, thanks to their long experience, their constantly improved instruments and the excellence of their methods, produce a heat capable of fully satisfying any requirement. But the experience that previously emerged only at the very tip of each white hair and that now emerges three months before they begin to put down roots, has taught them to avoid dangerous moments, and to overcome difficulties with dignity by simply sliding two insulating parts against each other, thus producing an effective and permanent protection for their intimate climatic properties and reducing all attacks to nothing. Joseph, sure of himself, followed Rosemary into the centre of the rainforest and went down with her into the depths of the lost cavern. There, as could have been foreseen, an argument broke out.

"I'm telling you, that's no old air-wolf," said Joseph. It's the future unknown soldier.

"Open your eyes," exclaimed Rosemarie scornfully, "there's no doubt that it's an old air-wolf; look how the pipe is smoking between its lips and how its hands are shaped like a forced landing."

"I don't see any such forced landing and, as for that pipe, it's nothing but a kite hanging from its mouth or, if you prefer, a kind of fiery vomit in which you can see a compass pointing to a time ninety years after the birth of Joseph. I maintain that it's the future unknown soldier; see how medals sprout from its nose and just look at its sarcastic smile."

"Impossible. If it were the future unknown soldier, it would show obvious signs of life. Besides, it would prove that there were still going to be wars which, as you know, is a serious scientific error."

"I never said that it's the unknown soldier from *our* future wars; don't take me for an imbecile. I tell you that's what it was going to be in the wars of men, and it could not realise its dream because death surprised it before the final war.

de los hombres, y no alcanzó a realizar su sueño, porque la muerte le sorprendió antes de la última guerra.

Para la perfecta comprensión de nuestra historia, debemos decir al atento lector que esta terrible discusión removió las fibras armoniosas del futuro soldado desconocido, el cual, despegando sus labios de mármol, dejó caer la pipa y cantó esta hermosa canción:

> Yo he visto dos ardillas
> Haciendo morisquetas
> Ordeñar un sepulcro
> Lanzando palanquetas
>
> Por qué razón el paraguas
> Ha bajado de los cielos
> Por qué razón las ardillas
> Se escobillan en sus vuelos
>
> Por qué la guerra que yo espero
> Se perdió en el bosque espeso

Después de entonada la última palabra, se oyó un disparo de cañón y un disparo de sombrero. Al mismo tiempo, toda la caverna se llenó de estalactitas de honor.

Por la misma razón, Rose Marie sobrepasó la medida de un metro y se convirtió en Carolina, lo cual obligó a José a salir con ella fuera de la caverna y conducirla hacia un Antonio que sería entonces más propio para ella, pues sabido es que los Antonios deben casar con Carolinas y los José con Rose Maries.

Carolina y Antonio se abrazaron llorando de alegría en medio de un llano que giraba en torno de su eje, como una hoja a merced de las poleas del viento que pasa sin saludar.

En esos momentos de amor, una deplorable regresión hacia los tiempos históricos apareció en esos seres revolucionados y posthistóricos. Lágrimas con pelos les brotaban desde el interior de sus glóbulos, termómetros de savia ascendían en torbellino por el magma de sus cuerpos. Se frotaban sus glóbulos con un ruido que casi recordaba los antiguos besos y en una fiebre de fidelidad, catorce flechas alfa les atravesaron de parte a parte, produciéndoles un deleite desconocido e intraducible.

So that our story might be perfectly understood, we must inform the attentive reader that this terrible argument stirred the harmonious fibres of the future unknown soldier who, peeling off his marble lips, dropped his pipe and sang this beautiful song:

> I've seen two squirrels
> Singing funny songs
> Milking a tombstone
> Hurling hammer and tongs
>
> Oh why did the umbrella
> Fall down from the sky
> And why do the squirrels
> Brush themselves when they fly
>
> Why did the war that I long for
> Get lost on the dense forest floor

After the last word had been sung, a cannon shot was heard, and a hat shot too. At the same time, the entire cavern was filled with stalactites of honour.

For the same reason, Rosemary's height went over the one metre mark and she turned into a Caroline, which forced Joseph to take her out of the cave and lead her to one of the Antonys, who would be a better match for her, since we all know that Antonys have to marry Carolines and Josephs have to marry Rosemarys.

Caroline and Antony embraced, weeping with joy in the midst of a plain that revolved around its axis, like a leaf at the mercy of the pulleys of a wind passing though, greeting no-one as it does so.

In those moments of love, a deplorable regression to historic times appeared in those revolutionised and post-historic beings. Hairy tears gushed from inside their globules; thermometers of sap rose, whirling up through the magma of their bodies. They rubbed their globules together with a noise almost reminiscent of old kisses and in a fever of fidelity, fourteen alpha arrows pierced them one by one, granting them an unknown and untranslatable delight.

Carolina, mirando a José con un aire atlántico, exclamó:

—Disculpa, José, yo no puedo amarte, pues tú eres varios y yo me he convertido en exclusivista.

José permaneció mudo y clavado en el suelo como una lámpara de amargura, con las orejas radioactivas vueltas hacia el horizonte. Ante ese espectáculo de ternura incomparable, se sintió cogido por un rayo ultratango que le lanzó al espacio contra un eclipse y se rompió en mil pedazos.

Un gran relámpago salido de las alturas se alejó creciendo como el más bello juramento de amor.

Para la perfecta comprensión de nuestra historia, aquí debemos terminar nuestra historia.

Caroline, looking at Joseph with an Atlantic air, exclaimed:

"Forgive me, Joseph, I cannot love you, because you are many and I have become an exclusivist."

Joseph stayed mute, fixed to the ground like a lamp of bitterness, his radioactive ears turned towards the horizon. Faced with this spectacle of incomparable tenderness, he felt himself caught by an ultratango ray that hurled him into space against an eclipse and he broke into a thousand pieces.

A great lightning bolt that came from on high receded, growing like the most beautiful declaration of love.

So that our story might be perfectly understood, we should end our story here.

EL JARDINERO
DEL CASTILLO DE MEDIANOCHE

(Novela policial)

Al oír un grito desesperado, los vecinos corrieron a la casa vecina. La puerta y las ventanas estaban cerradas. La puerta fue violentada, y al pasar el umbral los vecinos quedaron petrificados por el horrible cuadro que apareció ante sus ojos. Un cadáver estaba allí tendido con la boca abierta y los brazos más abiertos aún. Debido a su pequeño acento de *sale étranger*, se podía adivinar que la víctima era un suizo.

A fuerza de largas investigaciones, se llegó a la conclusión de que el cadáver presente, no había muerto de muerte natural, sino que había sido asesinado por un ser misterioso. Se veía sobre la punta de su lengua la extraña picadura de un animal o de un insecto, tal vez un escorpión hipnotizado por el inmundo criminal.

No era difícil percibir en la habitación las señales de una lucha evidente. En el techo se veían clavadas las obras completas de Racine, Corneille y Moliere. El tintero estaba lleno de sangre; en la mano derecha de la víctima, crispada por la muerte, se encontraba una larga barba recién arrancada y en la mano izquierda una carta de visita con el nombre Félix Potin, escrito dentro de un triángulo rojo.

Los vecinos corrieron en busca de la policía. Al volver acompañados de dos jueces, cinco detectives y catorce policías, encontraron el departamento en perfecto orden y arrendado al Sr. Charles Dupont, honrado representante viajero del Dépôt Nicolas.

Los policías estaban desconcertados, cuando de pronto uno de los dos detectives aficionados mostró a los tres detectives profesionales la silueta de un hermoso yate que pasaba flotando, como a la deriva sobre el Támesis. El yate llevaba entre sus labios una magnífica pipa que todos reconocieron en el acto, como la pipa del célebre detective Alfonso Trece.

Como el lector debe de haber comprendido, Jorge Quinto acababa de ser asesinado. ¿Quién le había asesinado? ¿Eran acaso los boy scouts ingleses? ¿Era la mano negra de carbón de los carbonarios italianos? ¿Era tal vez la Legión de Honor polonesa? Pero ¿cómo asegurarlo? Se necesitaba aclarar el misterio antes de lanzar a los cuatro vientos semejante acusación.

THE GARDENER
FROM THE CASTLE OF MIDNIGHT

(Detective novel)

On hearing a desperate scream, the neighbours ran to the neighbouring house. The door and the windows were closed. They forced the door but, as they crossed the threshold, the neighbours stopped, petrified by the horrible sight that met their eyes. A corpse was lying there, its mouth wide open and its arms even wider. Because of his slight *dirty foreigner's* accent, it was deduced that the victim was Swiss.

After a long investigation, it was concluded that the corpse in question had not died a natural death, but had been killed by a mysterious being. On the tip of his tongue one could see the peculiar bite of an animal or an insect, perhaps a scorpion hypnotized by the filthy criminal.

It was not difficult to detect signs of obvious struggle in the room. The complete works of Racine, Corneille and Molière could be seen nailed to the ceiling. The inkwell was full of blood; in the victim's right hand, stiff with *rigor mortis*, there was a long beard that had recently been torn off, and in his left hand there was a visiting card bearing the name of Woolworth, written inside a red triangle.

The neighbours ran out in search of the police. On returning, accompanied by two judges, five detectives and fourteen policemen, they found the apartment in perfect order and rented out to Mr. Charles Dupont, upstanding travelling salesman for a wine merchant.

The police were baffled, when suddenly one of the two amateur detectives pointed out to the three professional detectives the silhouette of a beautiful yacht that was floating past, as if adrift on the Thames. The yacht bore between its lips a magnificent pipe that everyone instantly recognized as the one belonging to the famous detective Alfonso Thirteen.

As the reader must have gathered, George V had just been assassinated. Who had assassinated him? Were they perchance English boy-scouts? Was it the carbon-black hand of the Italian Carbonari? Was it perhaps the Polish Legion of Honour? But how to be sure? The mystery had to be cleared up before such an accusation could be hurled to the four winds.

El perro lobo, consciente de su deber, se puso una barba y sus anteojos de carey, cogió su pipa y un violín que había servido en otras ocasiones al célebre pintor Ingres. Así disfrazado, se lanzó en busca del asesino, Debernos advertir que ese disfraz le asemejaba de un modo perfecto al señor Charles Dupont en persona.

Guillermo Segundo, más muerto que vivo, se lanzó también por su cuenta en busca del criminal. Quería descifrar el misterio, fuere como fuere, o acaso alejar de su persona toda sospecha. Detrás de cada oreja llevaba una bandera de la Legión de Honor polonesa (esto para inspirar confianza a los maliciosos). Sobre la cabeza llevaba un saco de sardinas noruegas y bajo sus pies almohadones de plumas verdes. Así, perfectamente ataviado, se lanzó a todo galope tras la pista del asesino.

Se veían pasar a una velocidad diabólica y moderna toda clase de motocicletas, una detrás de otra, doscientos automóviles, sesenta y siete aeroplanos, perros policías, palomas mensajeras, caballos árabes, varios hábiles skieurs, tortugas privadas de Scotland Yard, langostas fritas de la rue de Saussais, etc. Todas las policías del mundo habían sido movilizadas. Teléfono, y telégrafos no descansaban un momento enviándose señales sobre el presunto asesino. Los periódicos de todos los países estaban llenos de detalles del horrible crimen y chorreaban sangre de la víctima.

La sombra del asesino se deslizaba por todas partes, pero permanecía en las sombras. El miedo había invadido los hogares. Las mujeres rompían el entablado de los pisos para esconder la cabeza, los niños se mecían en las más altas lámparas y lloraban sin cesar toda la noche, llamando a los papás que habían subido sobre los tejados a escrutar el horizonte. Sólo las sirvientas, esas muchachas desnaturalizadas, se dejaban violar por los palomos mensajeros en sus jaulas doradas.

Era una bella noche de verano. La luna de Austerlitz brillaba en el cielo. El jardinero Schiller había entrado aquella tarde en el castillo con el pretexto de cortar muebles y barrer los caminillos y los árboles. Para no ser reconocido y tener un aire inocente se había vestido de Père Noël. A cada paso que daba se volvía hacia atrás receloso y barría sus pisadas con un erizo de los mares del sur. A veces levantaba la cabeza y hacía signos luminosos con un cuerno de caza. De pronto se oyó el eco de una respuesta lejana y casi al mismo instante se abrió una ventana del cuarto piso y un canguro entró en la habitación de la marquesa, la cual lo mismo que el canguro estaba disfrazada de policía internacional. Se oyó un grito desesperado, siniestro, que salía del subterráneo. El canguro y la marquesa

The wolfhound, aware of his duty, donned a beard and his tortoise-shell glasses and took up his pipe, and a violin that had been used on other occasions by the famous painter Ingres. Thus disguised, he set off in search of the murderer. We should point out that this disguise gave him an exact resemblance to Mr. Charles Dupont himself.

Wilhelm II, more dead than alive, also set off on his own in search of the criminal. Be that as it may, he wished to solve the mystery or perhaps just remove all suspicion from himself. Behind each ear he wore the ribbon of the Polish Legion of Honour (this, so as to inspire confidence in malicious persons). On his head he bore a sack of Norwegian sardines, and beneath his feet cushions filled with green feathers. Thus perfectly attired, he galloped off on the trail of the murderer.

One after the other, all kinds of motorcycles, two hundred cars, sixty-seven aeroplanes, police dogs, carrier pigeons, Arabian horses, several skilful skiers, private turtles from Scotland Yard, fried lobsters from the rue de Saussais, etc. were seen to pass by at a diabolical and modern speed. Every policeman in the world had been mobilised. Telephones and telegraphs did not rest for a moment, sending signals to each other concerning the alleged murderer. Newspapers in every country were filled with details of the horrible crime and dripped with the blood of the victim.

The shadow of the murderer slipped here and there, but remained in the shadows. Fear had invaded homes. Women broke the floorboards to hide their heads; children were rocked in the highest lamps and cried ceaselessly all night, calling out to their fathers who had climbed onto the roof to examine the horizon. Only the maids, those perverted girls, let themselves be ravished by carrier pigeons in their golden cages.

It was a beautiful summer night. The moon of Austerlitz shone in the sky. Schiller the gardener had entered the castle that afternoon on the pretext of cutting furniture and sweeping the paths and trees. To avoid recognition, and so as to maintain an air of innocence, he came disguised as Santa Claus. After every step he looked back suspiciously and swept his footprints with an urchin from the South Seas. Sometimes he lifted his head and made lighted signals with a hunting horn. Suddenly there was the echo of a distant reply, and almost at the same moment a window on the fourth floor opened and a kangaroo entered the chamber of the Marchioness who, like the kangaroo, was disguised as an international policeman. There was a desperate, sinister scream from the lower reaches of the castle. The kangaroo and the Marchioness fell senseless without

cayeron desmayados antes de proferir una sola palabra. El jardinero exhaló una especie de gemido en su cuerno de caza, y una paloma mensajera le entregó un papel plegado con tres líneas escritas a máquina.

Dos ojos escondidos detrás de una cueva de ratones seguían ávidamente todos los movimientos del jardinero. La luna de Austerlitz bajaba en el ciclo, y un lacayo imitando a Lloyd George y a Woodrow Wilson, atravesaba un sendero del jardín llevando un ramo de orquídeas y profiriendo grandes palabras. Los ojos escondidos que seguían esta escena sin perder un detalle, se cerraron de repente y aparecieron mirando por el ojo de la cerradura de la caja de caudales del Leviatán que subía por el canal grande de Venecia, rodeado de canciones de mandolina. Los ojos misteriosos volvieron a cerrarse y aparecieron otra vez en la cueva de ratas del Castillo de Medianoche. La marquesa no había aún vuelto de su viaje y el canguro seguía durmiendo sobre su hermosa cama Luis XV. Luis Quince tornaba desayuno en la pieza del lado, rodeado del jardinero y de sus doce hermanos, todos disfrazados de santos de nieve. Uno a uno fueron levantándose y golpeando por turno con un martillo una gran campana de plata. Así sonaron doce campanadas. El último, viendo que no había más campanadas en la campana, abrió la ventana y se lanzó al vacío.

Después de haber seguido estas escenas, los ojos misteriosos se cerraron en la cueva de las ratas y se abrieron al fondo de un obscuro corredor del Vaticano.

El Cardenal Pitelli gritaba a voz en cuello:

—Atrás, infames. No tenéis vergüenza, cinco contra uno. A mí, caballeros. Aquí la guardia suiza. Diez puñales traidores sobre el Papa, Corred, corred.

Una hora más tarde, los periódicos de Italia anunciaban en grandes titulares, la triste nueva: "Dos metecos: un francés y un turcomano, seguidos de varios secuaces, han asesinado al Santo Padre."

Los ojos misteriosos, después de presenciar la tremenda tragedia y de leer su confirmación en los diarios, se cerraron más rápidos que nunca y volvieron a abrirse detrás de un reloj en forma de triángulo de Salomón, en el salón secreto del Gran Oriente Internacional. Siete ancianos, metidos en largas togas de fantasma, discutían en voz baja sobre un mapa del mundo.

—Señores, debemos bajar del Himalaya a las doce de la noche y presentarnos de sorpresa, cuando nadie pueda sospechar…

—Aprobado.

—Aprobado.

uttering a single word. The gardener let out a kind of groan into his hunting horn and a carrier pigeon passed him a folded piece of paper bearing three typewritten lines.

Two eyes hidden behind a mouse-hole eagerly followed the gardener's every move. The moon of Austerlitz carried on waning and a lackey, in the manner of Lloyd George and Woodrow Wilson, crossed a garden path carrying a bunch of orchids and uttering grand words. The hidden eyes that followed this scene, missing not one single detail, suddenly closed and reappeared looking through the keyhole of the treasure chest of Leviathan, which was going up Venice's Grand Canal, to the accompaniment of mandolin songs. The mysterious eyes closed again and then reappeared in a rat hole in the Castle of Midnight. The Marchioness had not yet returned from her journey and the kangaroo was still sleeping on a beautiful Louis XV bed. Louis XV was having breakfast in the next room, surrounded by the gardener and his twelve brothers, all disguised as snow saints. One by one they got up and in turn struck a great silver bell with a hammer. That's why twelve chimes rang out. The final brother, seeing that there were no more chimes left in the bell, opened the window and threw himself into thin air.

After watching these scenes, the mysterious eyes closed in the rat hole and opened again at the end of a dark corridor in the Vatican.

Cardinal Pitelli was bellowing loudly:

"Get back, you villains! Five against one! Have you no shame? To me, gentlemen. Fetch the Swiss Guard. Ten traitorous daggers raised over the Pope. Run, run."

One hour later, the Italian newspapers announced the sad news in great headlines: "Two foreigners, a Frenchman and a Turcoman, followed by several henchmen, have assassinated the Holy Father."

The mysterious eyes, after witnessing the terrible tragedy and reading confirmation of it in the newspapers, closed quicker than ever and reopened behind a clock in the form of Solomon's triangle, in the secret hall of the Grand Orient International. Seven old men in long ghostly robes were arguing quietly over a map of the world.

"Gentlemen, we must come down from the Himalayas at midnight and pretend to be surprised, so that no one will suspect…"

"Agreed."

"Agreed."

—Eso es, presentarnos de sorpresa.

—Bajeremos del Himalaya en bicicletas silenciosas y perfumadas, a las doce de la noche.

Apenas oídas estas palabras, los ojos misteriosos le cerraron y un minuto después se abrían en la cueva de las ratas, en el jardín del Castillo.

Un árbol inmenso había crecido en medio del jardín. Se oía un ruido extraño en el interior del árbol. Evidentemente no era el ruido musical de la savia, pues a veces se oían vagos gemidos y las ramas se estremecían sacudidas por largos sollozos.

El jardinero Schiller miraba inquieto hacia todos lados. De pronto se acercó al árbol y murmuró:

—Querido Goethe, ¡que me importa a mí el Papa! He aquí la cuerda con la cual le habían atado. Un trocito de esta cuerda trae buena suerte, e la puedo dejar, como último precio, en dieciocho francos.

Al mismo tiempo, el rostro de la marquesa apareció en el balcón y se volvió al interior gritando:

—Un aerolito, un aerolito. Absalón, Absalón, un aerolito.

—Lo vi — respondió una voz dura —; los francmasones, ya te he dicho, los francmasones.

Oyendo estos gritos, los ojos misteriosos vieron abrirse el piano de cola y caer un ancla, que se clavó en el fondo de la alfombra. Una sirena silbó desde el piano, e inmediatamente después se oyó golpear las puertas y el ruido de pasos, subiendo las escaleras y recorriendo los corredores. Los ojos misteriosos vieron abrirse la puerta y un ciento de canguros vestidos con el uniforme azul horizonte de los soldados franceses, desaparecieron en el piano. ¿Era ésta la armada gloriosa que había combatido bajo las órdenes del rey Dagoberto en Poitiers sur Seine? La gloriosa armada bajó las escaleras del piano que conducían a dos pies mecánicos, los cuales formaban los cimientos del Castillo de Medianoche. Cuando los canguros llegaron por el interior a los dedos de los pies que eran largos como Broadway y llenos de bares y cabarets luminosos, las piernas empezaron a andar.

Los cabellos de los ojos misteriosos se pusieron de punta ante tal espectáculo y los ojos se cerraron para abrirse casi instantáneamente en la cueva de ratas del jardín. Vieron el mar y las palmeras y oían los gritos de los croupiers de Montecarlo: *Faites vos jeux, faites vos jeux.*

El oro inglés corría sobre las mesas y compraba todas las ciencias.

A orillas del mar se veía desembarcar cien maletas, en las cuales se encontraban los cadáveres, aún palpitantes, de los cien canguros

"That's right, let's make our appearance a surprise."

"We'll come down from the Himalayas at midnight, on silent, perfumed bicycles."

Scarcely had these words been heard than the mysterious eyes closed only to reopen a minute later in the rat hole, in the castle garden.

A huge tree had grown in the middle of the garden. There was a strange noise from inside the tree. Clearly it was not the musical sound of sap, for sometimes there were groans and the branches shook with long sobs.

Schiller the gardener looked anxiously all around him. Suddenly he approached the tree and murmured:

"Dear Goethe, I don't care about the Pope! Here's the rope they tied him up with. A little piece of this rope brings good luck, and I can let you have it for eighteen francs, final price."

At the same moment, the Marchioness's face appeared on the balcony and she went back inside shouting:

"A meteorite, a meteorite. Absalom, Absalom, a meteorite."

"I saw it," replied a harsh voice; "it's the Freemasons; I've told you before, it's the Freemasons."

Hearing these cries, the mysterious eyes saw the grand piano open and an anchor fall out, burying itself deep in the carpet. A siren whistled from the piano and, straight afterwards, there came the sound of doors banging and of feet going up stairs and along corridors. The mysterious eyes saw the door open and a hundred kangaroos dressed in the horizon-blue uniform of French soldiers disappeared into the piano. Was this the glorious army that had fought under the orders of King Dagobert at Poitiers-sur-Seine? The glorious army descended the piano's stairs leading to two mechanical feet, which formed the foundations of the Castle of Midnight. When the kangaroos came through the interior to the toes on these feet, which were as long as Broadway and filled with brightly-lit bars and cabarets, the legs began to move.

Such a spectacle made the hair of the mysterious eyes stand on end and the eyes closed, only to open almost immediately in the garden rat hole. They saw the sea and the palm trees and heard the calls of the Monte Carlo croupiers: *Faites vos jeux, faites vos jeux.*

English gold flowed over the tables and bought all the sciences.

On the seashore a hundred suitcases were seen disembarking; these contained the still palpitating corpses of the one hundred kangaroos

recientemente asesinados por orden de los jesuítas.

La marquesa con un cinismo de princesa prusiana, se sentó al piano y cantó el Foxtrot funerario de Schubert.

El kaiser de Montecarlo, apareció vestido de sacerdote egipcio, cogió las cien maletas, las cargó sobre otros tantos aviones, los cuales después de haber girado tres veces en torno al faro, volaron hacia Moscú.

Los ojos misteriosos se cerraron ante este cuadro doloroso, para abrirse en un cajón del escritorio del Jefe del Guepeú.

Stalin salía del Kremlin. Por entre los barrotes del tragaluz subterráneo, lanzó un queso, envuelto en un número del *Intran* al último Romanoff, que, atraído por el fuerte olor del periódico, corrió al paquete, abrió el queso y se sentó a leer ávidamente un artículo admirable sobre la pintura francesa.

Los ojos misteriosos se cerraron con un suspire desolado y se abrieron detrás de la tercera máscara negra del Museo del Trocadéro de París.

Ante un magnífico monolito de la isla de Pascua, el General de los jesuitas, explicaba a la mariscala Citroën, la horrible lucha de los misioneros contra los indígenas en las islas del Pacífico y cómo los jesuitas se habían devorado a los últimos antropófagos.

Se veían pasar por las salas en traje de gran gala y unos en pos de otros, diversos personajes y personalidades del nuevo mundo literario y artístico. Todos los célebres Antonios desfilaron ante los ojos misteriosos: Mrs. Antoine Duchamp, Antoine Schoenberg, Antoine Matisse, Antoine Picasso, Antoine Picabia, Antoine Braque, Antoine Strawinsky, Antoine Brancusi, Antoine Mondrian, Antoine Eluard, Antoine Lipchitz, Antoine Torres García, Antoine Miró, Antoine Masson, Antoine Aragon, Antoine Varèse, Antoine Ernest, Antoine Vitrac, Antoine Léger, Antoine Tzara, Antoine Gleizes, Antoine Breton, Antoine Klee, Antoine Crével, Antoine Hélion, Antoine Gropius, Antoine Laurens, Antoine Jolas, Antoine Giacommetti, Antoine Calder, Antoine Corbusier, Antoinette Dreier, Antoine Sima, Antoine Daumal, Antoinette Doesbourg, Antoinette Taeuber, Antoine Marcoussis, Antoine Kandinsky, Antoine Chagall, Antoine Zervos y los Antoines de los Antoines: Antoine Huidobro y Antoine Arp, que se distinguían por el alto talle de sus ojos, la elegancia de sus dientes, la lucidez de sus cabellos.

De pronto la mariscala Citroën y el General de los Jesuítas dejaron caer sus ropas y pudo verse que la mariscala Citroën era el General de los Jesuitas y que el General de los Jesuítas era la mariscala Citroën. Pero

recently murdered by order of the Jesuits.

The Marchioness, with the cynicism of a Prussian princess, sat at the piano and sang Schubert's funeral foxtrot.

The Kaiser of Monte Carlo appeared, clad as an Egyptian priest, took the one hundred suitcases, loaded them onto as many planes which, after making three circuits of the lighthouse, flew in the direction of Moscow.

The mysterious eyes closed before this painful picture, to open in a desk drawer of the head of the GPU.

Stalin was leaving the Kremlin. He threw a cheese wrapped in a copy of *L'Intran* through the bars of the basement skylight, to the last Romanov who, attracted by the strong smell from the newspaper, ran to the package, opened the cheese and sat down to read avidly a fine article on French painting.

The mysterious eyes closed with a desolate sigh and opened behind the third black mask in the Trocadéro Museum in Paris.

In front of a magnificent monolith from Easter Island, the Jesuit General was explaining to the wife of Marshall Citroën the missionaries' horrible struggle against the native peoples of the Pacific islands and how the Jesuits had devoured the last cannibals.

One could see persons and personalities from the new literary and artistic world passing one after the other through the halls in grand gala costumes. All the famous Antonys paraded before the mysterious eyes: Messrs. Antoine Duchamp, Antoine Schoenberg, Antoine Matisse, Antoine Picasso, Antoine Picabia, Antoine Braque, Antoine Stravinsky, Antoine Brancusi, Antoine Mondrian, Antoine Eluard, Antoine Lipchitz, Antoine Torres García, Antoine Miró, Antoine Masson, Antoine Aragon, Antoine Varèse, Antoine Ernest, Antoine Vitrac, Antoine Léger, Antoine Tzara, Antoine Gleizes, Antoine Breton, Antoine Klee, Antoine Crével, Antoine Hélion, Antoine Gropius, Antoine Laurens, Antoine Jolas, Antoine Giacommetti, Antoine Calder, Antoine Corbusier, Antoinette Dreier, Antoine Sima, Antoine Daumal, Antoinette Doesbourg, Antoinette Taeuber, Antoine Marcoussis, Antoine Kandinsky, Antoine Chagall, Antoine Zervos and the Antoines of Antoines: Antoine Huidobro and Antoine Arp, who were distinguished by the size of their eyes, the elegance of their teeth, the brightness of their hair.

Suddenly the wife of Marshall Citroën and the Jesuit General dropped their clothes and it could be seen that Marshall Citroën's wife was the General of the Jesuits and that the General of the Jesuits was

observando con mayor atención, se pudo afirmar que ambos no eran sino el único y famoso jardinero del Castillo de Medianoche.

Entonces, en medio del silencio y de la consternación general, el jardinero gritó:

—Los Antoines, firmes.

Les hizo colocarse todos en dos filas regulares y todos partieron al son de una marcha militar.

Somos los Antoines y las Antoinettes.
Somos los sobrinos de Mistinguette.

Ante esta triste escena los ojos misteriosos se separaron indignados. El de la derecha partió al Brasil para hacerse plantador de café, y el de la izquierda cogió un taxi y se hizo conducir a la plaza de la República.

Viendo desaparecer a lo lejos los ojos misteriosos siguiendo su destino, en lo más alto de la Torre Eiffel tres voces discutían a grandes gritos:

—Es el Papa Negro.

—No, son los francmasones.

—Probaré que son los bolcheviques.

Pero habiendo desaparecido los ojos misteriosos que seguían los crímenes, los crímenes también desaparecieron y todas las madres de familia pudieron dormir tranquilas.

Marshall Citroën's wife. But on closer observation, it could be confirmed that both were none other than the unique, famous gardener from the Castle of Midnight.

Then, amidst the silence and general consternation, the gardener cried out:

"Antoines, stand to attention."

He made them all stand in two straight lines and they all left to the sound of a military march.

We are the Antoines and the Antoinettes.
We're nephews and nieces of Mistinguette.

Confronted with this sad scene the mysterious eyes each went their own way indignantly. The one on the right went to Brazil to become a coffee planter, and the one on the left took a taxi and was driven to the Place de la République.

Seeing the mysterious eyes vanish into the distance, each following its own destiny, at the very top of the Eiffel Tower three voices argued loudly:

"It's the Black Pope."

"No, it's the Freemasons."

"I'll prove it's the Bolsheviks."

But as the mysterious eyes that followed the crimes had disappeared, the crimes also disappeared, and all housewives could now sleep peacefully.

LA CIGÜEÑA ENCADENADA

(Novela patriótica y alsaciana)

La Alsacia, como su nombre lo indica, es un país llamado a los más altos destinos. Es el país más limpio del mundo; cambia sus camisas sucias cada treinta años. Digiere sus banderas como su exquisito Paté de Foie de piano, célebre en toda la tierra. Su delicioso queso oliente a violín Stradivarius, su Munster de Luna creciente sirve como brújula para encontrar en las capas geológicas del mundo la raza *poloise*, tan conocida por el *esprit polois*.

De estas capas geológicas propias, ellos importan en toneles su lengua *poloise* y las nudos de corbata cabezal de las campesinas alsacianas, sólo llevados por Madame Chenille en las grandes ocasiones de las grandes guerras.

Aunque los cigüeñenses comieron durante un tiempo el imponderable Paté de niños belgas, no han perdido, sin embargo, la pureza de su lengua *poloise*, en la cual, desde los tiempos de César como todos sabéis en vez de *sí* se dice *ya,* y en vez de *no* se dice *nein*.

—Ya, ya, nein, nein gritaba la voz sonora de Hans Gunter, que se paseaba con su fusil cazando jabalíes sobre las cornisas y entre las gárgolas de la catedral de Estrasburgo.

El pobre Hans erró el último disparo, y en vez de matar un jabalí de dos toneladas y media, mató un magnífico cuadro bíblico del gran pintor Henner. El cuadro que se alejaba flotando sobre el río Yll, recibió el tiro en pleno corazón, pero como estaba firmado Herman Chatriam, se pudo ver que era un himno musical. Ayudado de un imán, Hans Gunter lo sacó del agua y sirviéndose de la respiración artificial de repetidos masajes e inyecciones de coramina, pudo volverlo a la vida. Su primera palabra al reabrir los ojos fue una pregunta angustiada:

—¿Cómo está mi madre patria?

Pero como Hans Gunter sólo comprendía el *polois,* respondió:

—Ya, ya, Berlín es una gran ciudad.

—No— contestó el polígrota herido—, yo pregunto por Babilonia. Quisiera saber si los tigres de bengala o los fuegos fatuos han devorado a

THE STORK IN CHAINS

(Patriotic and Alsatian novel)

Alsace, as its name suggests, is a country called to the highest of destinies. It is the cleanest country in the world; it changes its dirty shirts every thirty years. It swallows its flags like its exquisite world-famous piano liver pâté. Its delicious cheese smells like a Stradivarius violin; its crescent-moon Munster serves as a compass for locating in the world's geological layers the *Saintpolist* race, so renowned for its *Saintpolist* wit.

From these very geological layers, they import by the barrel their *Saintpolist* tongue and the tie-knots on the heads of Alsatian peasant women, which only Madame Chenille wore on the grand occasion of great wars.

Although for a while the Storkists ate the priceless pâté of Belgian children, they did not however lose the purity of their *Saintpolist* language, in which, from the time of Caesar – as you all know – instead of *yes* they say *ja*, and instead of *no* they say *nein*.

"Ja, ja, nein, nein," shouted the sonorous voice of Hans Gunter, who was out with his rifle, hunting wild boar along the cornices and amongst the gargoyles of Strasbourg Cathedral.

Poor Hans missed his last shot, and instead of a two-and-a-half-ton wild boar, he killed a magnificent biblical painting by the great painter Henner. The painting, which floated away down the River Ill, took the shot right in the heart but, as it was signed by Erckmann-Chatrian, one could see it was a musical hymn. Aided by a magnet, Hans Gunter pulled it out of the water and, by applying artificial respiration – using repeated massages and injections of coramine – was able to resuscitate it. Its first words when it reopened its eyes were an anxious question:

"How is my motherland?"

But since Hans Gunter only understood *Saintpolist*, he replied:

"Yes, yes, Berlin is a great city."

"No," replied the wounded polyglot, "I'm asking after Babylon. I would like to know if Bengal tigers or will 'o the wisps have devoured the

la Ciudad Luz."[1]

Apenas pronunciadas estas palabras, la Ciudad Luz, a caballo sobre un arco de triunfo alazán llegó a todo galope.

—Bonjour, Monsieur et Dame. ¿Ustedes hablaban de mi, Monsieur et Dame? ¿No es verdad Mr. et Dame?

Hans Gunter, para hacerse entender mejor, respondió en latín:

—Aquí no hay Monsieur et Dame; sólo hay bosques y catedrales domésticas.

La selva, con las manos encadenadas por el agresor, pedía auxilio. Entonces la catedral, Hans Gunter, la Ciudad Luz y el polígloto herido se pusieron sus hermosos monóculos en el ojo derecho y vieron la terrible batalla que se libraba no lejos de allí, como de costumbre.

La batalla de Hastings ardía y tronaba. El señor Hastings en persona dirigía el combate. Tres capas de cadáveres cubrían el suelo. Cada capa estaba separada de la otra por una rebanada de jamón. Grandes olas de heroísmo montaban hacia las nubes amenazando con tragarse todos los teatros y los barcos que huían bajo las órdenes del capitán Aníbal y el teniente Nelson.

Para un noble corazón de soldado, era algo admirable ver cómo el viejo general Moltke ponía en fuga a los mámaros. Huían dando gritos de bailarinas diplomadas. Entretanto el pequeño caporal que acababa de desembarcar de la isla de los Cisnes con tres regimientos de soldados, aún no desconocidos, atacó violentamente la falange de elefantes blancos de Cayo Graco.

Moltke empezó a retirarse protegido por la flota de Coligny. El asalto a la bayoneta de nuestros valientes trescientos mil alpinos, apoyados por nuestros incomparables 68 y la caballería de nuestros invencibles meridionales, había empezado a las seis de la mañana. A las siete llegaban nuestros heroicos diablos amarillos, seguidos de cerca por nuestros indomables tirolianos. La Legión Extranjera, compuesta de miles de inmundos metecos, había perdido todos sus extranjeros. En su sitio, el general Hernán Cortés

---

[1] [*Nota de los autores*] La Ciudad Luz era célebre por sus luces, por sus W. C. ultramodernos, un hoyo en el suelo, sobre el cual se hace caca en equilibrio o planeando, como conviene en este siglo del deporte y la aviación, por la avaricia de los extranjeros y la generosidad de sus hijos, por la estupidez de los extranjeros y la inteligencia de sus hijos y sus nietos, por sus ascensores, siempre en *Arrêt Momentané,* esos ascensores en los cuales sólo cabía la dueña de la casa y la mitad de su marido, tan diferentes de los otros ascensores de rastacueros, donde caben dos o tres familias, etc.

City of Light.[1]

Hardly had these words been uttered, than the City of Light galloped up, mounted on a chestnut Arc de Triomphe.

"*Bonjour, Monsieur et Madame.* You were speaking of me, *Monsieur et Madame?* Isn't that right, *Monsieur et Madame?*"

Hans Gunter, to ensure he would be understood, replied in Latin:

"There's no *Monsieur et Madame* here; there's nothing but woodlands and domestic cathedrals."

The forest, its hands chained by the aggressor, begged for help. Then the cathedral, Hans Gunter, the City of Light and the wounded polyglot inserted fine monocles into their right eyes and saw the terrible battle being fought not far from there, as usual.

The Battle of Hastings blazed and thundered. Mr. Hastings himself led the fight. Three layers of corpses covered the ground. Each layer was separated from the next by a slice of ham. Great waves of heroism rose towards the clouds, threatening to swallow up all the theatres and ships that were fleeing under the command of Captain Hannibal and Lieutenant Nelson.

It did the noble heart of a soldier good to see old General Moltke putting the Mammarists to flight. They fled screaming like trained dancers. Meanwhile, the little corporal who had just disembarked from the Isle of Swans with three regiments of as-yet-unknown soldiers, violently attacked the phalanx of white elephants under Caius Gracchus.

Moltke began to withdraw, protected by Coligny's fleet. The onslaught with bayonets by our three hundred thousand brave Alpine troops, supported by our unbeatable 68th and the cavalry of our invincible southerners, had begun at six in the morning. At seven o'clock our heroic Yellow Devils arrived, closely followed by our indomitable Tyroleans. The Foreign Legion, consisting of thousands of filthy aliens, had lost all its foreigners. In their place, General Hernán Cortés had positioned our

---

[1] [*Authors' note*] The City of Light was famous for its lights, for its ultra-modern WCs – holes in the ground, where one poops while balancing, or while gliding, as is appropriate in this century of sports and aviation – for the greed of foreigners and generosity of its children, for the stupidity of foreigners and the intelligence of its children and grandchildren, for its elevators – forever in *temporary stoppage* – those elevators into which only the lady of the house and half of her husband could fit, so different from other upstart elevators, which can accommodate two or three families, etc.

había colocado nuestra intrépida Legión de Honor.

El cañón tronaba, un diluvio de balas caía desde cuarenta días y cuarenta noches, un muro de obuses avanzaba lentamente hacia el centro del mundo. Este muro estaba decorado con frescos y bajorrelieves de la gran época egipcia y algunos cuadros de batallas históricas para despertar el entusiasmo de nuestros valientes soldados. Por medio de rápidos ascensores, se subía hasta el punto culminante de la parábola descrita por nuestras balas y desde allí se podía contemplar el efecto desastroso que hacía nuestro fuego nutrido en las filas enemigas. Pequeños panteones flotaban en el aire y se veían frescas coronas y ramos de flores sobre las tumbas de mármol.

El políglota herido bostezó y luego contó a Hans Gunter que últimamente había visto en nuestra ilustre Babilonia una representación teatral en la Gran Opera a beneficio de los primeros mutilados de la guerra, en la cual se demostraba claramente que las provincias cautivas nos han amado siempre con el afecto sincero de su seguro servidor. Al levantarse el telón vimos dos cigüeñas encadenadas que después de haber oído un hermoso y maternal poema recitado por Madame Troisième Weber, vestida de Caterina (traje que representa a nuestra amada patria) lloraban amargamente. Sus lágrimas subían de punto o echaban punto al oír el verso que decía:

> *Hijas, he aquí mi pecho*
> *Os aguardo con los brazos abiertos.*

La señora Troisième Weber abría sus brazos mis grandes que la Australia y las dos cigüeñas encadenadas que, como el lector habrá comprendido, representaban las provincias cautivas que todo país posee en el extranjero, estallaron en gritos desolados, dirigiéndose a Madeleine (qué simboliza nuestra amada patria).

—Madre, libértanos, Madre, pronto volveremos a tu seno.

Después de esta delicada historia del políglota herido, la Ciudad Luz advirtió que era bastante difícil hacer comprender a los *polois* cautivos todas las amarguras que ella había sufrido.

De tiempo en tiempo se oía aún las voces de las cautivas:

—Madre, rompe nuestras cadenas. Mamá, libértanos del yugo extranjero.

—Mamá, queremos volver a tu seno tibio y perfumado.

La Ciudad Luz retiró su monóculo y dijo a sus amigos:

intrepid Legion of Honour.

Cannon thundered; a deluge of shells fell for forty days and forty nights. A wall of shells slowly advanced towards the centre of the world. This wall was decorated with frescos and bas-reliefs from the great Egyptian era, and some paintings of historic battles, to awaken the enthusiasm of our brave soldiers. By means of rapid elevators, one could climb to the topmost point of the parabola described by our shells and from there contemplate the disastrous effect our fire had on the enemy ranks. Little Pantheons floated in the air and fresh wreaths and bouquets of flowers could be seen on marble tombs.

The wounded polyglot yawned and then told Hans Gunter that he had recently seen a theatrical performance at the Great Opera in our illustrious Babylon for the benefit of the first war wounded, which clearly demonstrated that the captive provinces have always loved us with the sincere affection of a loyal servant. When the curtain rose we saw two chained storks weeping bitterly, after hearing a beautiful and maternal poem recited by Madame Troisième Weber, dressed as Catherine (a costume representing our beloved homeland). Their tears reached a climax upon hearing the verse which said:

> *Daughters, here is my breast*
> *I await you with open arms.*

Mrs Troisième Weber opened her arms wider than Australia, and the two chained storks which, as the reader will have understood, represented the captive provinces that every country possesses overseas, exploded into desolate cries, directed at Madeleine (who symbolizes our beloved homeland).

"Mother, set us free, Mother, we will soon return to your breast."

After this delicate story from the wounded polyglot, the City of Light warned that it was rather difficult to make the captive *Saintpolists* understand all the bitterness that it had suffered.

From time to time the voices of the captives could still be heard:

"Mother, break our chains. Mama, free us from the foreign yoke."

"Mama, we want to return to your warm and fragrant breast."

The City of Light took off its monocle and said to its friends:

"Los cigüeñenses nos han hecho sufrir tanto. Calla vez que queríamos explicarles nuestro martirio, respondían cantando la vieja canción de los turistas:

La Cigüeña e mobile
qual piuma al vento.

La catedral, Hans Gunter y los jabalíes lloraban sin consuelo al oír la historia de semejante dolor.

Volvían a oírse los gritos de las cautivas:

—Mamá, mamá, me hice pipí en los calzones. Los relojes de la Selva Negra y los quesos mámaros respondían: Cucú, cucú.

El políglota herido intervino ante los grandes escritores, Vicente Arp y Hans Huidobro, para suplicarles que no olvidaran el tono superior y noble que debe tener una historia histórica.

Todo lector de los periódicos *polois* sabe reconocer este tono por su olor a biombo y su sabor a limonada de salchichas gaseosas.

En vista de lo cual, los estimados artistas y queridos colegas Huidobro Arp y Hans Vicente arrancaron las piedras de nieve de sus ojos y las reemplazaron con oriflamas de lises y lotos que inmediatamente echaron raíces en ese buena tierra vegetal y crecieron como cuatro antenas recibiendo las ondas de valses guerreros y de las últimas batallas.

Nuestros heroicos soldados habían sido vencidos por los fugitivos mámaros. No hay ni qué decir que nosotros éramos superiores desde todo punto de vista. Nuestra inteligencia franca, clara, frente a la hipocresía habitual de los pesados mámaros que se vanagloriaban de ser capaces de vencernos en tres días con sus ochenta miserables cañones, punto de vista absolutamente falso y ridículo, pues fuimos vencidos en dos horas y por treinta cañones, lo que prueba su ignorancia estratégica. Los desgraciados vencedores ni siquiera supieron aprovecharse de su victoria. Apenas lograron destruirnos algunas plazas fuertes y tomarnos Londres, París, Berlin, Madrid, Roma, Viena y Praga. Nosotros conservamos siempre Concarneau, Albacete, Sorrento, Hull, Francfort, Delft y Montecarlo.

Con cuánta razón nuestros diarios hablaban del misterio inexplicable de la derrota. Nuestra superioridad de raza es indiscutible. La elegancia y la belleza de nuestras mujeres no tiene rival en parte alguna. El talento agudo de nuestros hombres, su esprit, ¿cómo puede compararse con la

"The Storkists have caused us much suffering. Whenever we tried to explain to them the nature of our martyrdom, they responded by singing the old tourist song:

> *La Cicogna e mobile*
> *qual piuma al vento.*[2]

The cathedral, Hans Gunter and the wild boars wept inconsolably at hearing such a tale of woe.

The cries of the captives were heard again:

"Mama, mama, I peed in my pants." The Black Forest clocks and the Mammarist cheeses replied, "Cuckoo, cuckoo."

The wounded polyglot intervened before the great writers Vicente Arp and Hans Huidobro, begging them not to forget the superior and noble tone appropriate to such a storied story.

Every reader of the *Saintpolist* newspapers can recognise that tone from its odour of room-dividers and its lemonade taste of gassy sausages.

In view of which, the esteemed artists and dear colleagues Huidobro Arp and Hans Vicente plucked the snowstones from their eyes and replaced them with oriflammes of lilies and lotus blossom that immediately took root in that good topsoil and grew like four antennae receiving broadcasts of warrior waltzes and the latest battles.

Our heroic soldiers had been defeated by the Mammarist fugitives, Needless to say we were superior, no matter how you look at it. Our frank, clear intelligence in the face of the habitual hypocrisy of the plodding Mammarists, who boasted of being able to defeat us within three days with their eighty miserable cannon – an absolutely false and ridiculous point of view, since we were defeated in two hours, and by thirty cannon, which is proof of their lack of strategic knowledge. The wretched winners did not even know how to take advantage of their victory. They barely managed to destroy some of our fortresses and only took from us London, Paris, Berlin, Madrid, Rome, Vienna and Prague. We still hold Concarneau, Albacete, Sorrento, Hull, Frankfurt, Delft and Monte Carlo.

How rightly our newspapers spoke of the inexplicable mystery of the

---

[2] *[Translator's note]* The author is playing here on the aria 'La donna è mobile' from Verdi's opera *Rigoletto*, the quoted lines meaning "Woman is fickle / Like a feather on the wind". Huidobro replaces "donna" with "cigüeña" (stork) and the "translation" above replaces this with the Italian word for stork, "cicogna".

inteligencia nebulosa y grasienta de los mámaros, de raza impura y sin tradiciones seculares? ¿Por qué razón fuimos vencidos? ¡Qué insondable misterio! ¿Por qué fuimos vencidos? ¿Fue a causa de la crisis financiera y artística? ¿Fue a causa de la falta de ejercicio metódico en nuestras tropas? ¿O acaso a causa de que nuestros soldados no habían tomado su aperitivo aquel día? Imposible explicarse la derrota. Ella quedará como una incógnita en la historia.

La catedral, Hans Gunter, la Ciudad Luz, el políglota herido y la Selva Negra bajaron de la plataforma de la catedral. A fuerza de dar vueltas y más vueltas, se convertían en carrouseles, de sus estómagos salía una música alegre e infernal, pequeños trineos les crecían en los callos de los pies y cientos de trompos giraban en torno de ellos. Se producían enormes torbellinos en los cuales los generales Aníbal, Nelson, Moltke, Pompeyo, Hernán Cortés, Napoleón, fueron devorados y salieron transformados en ojales con rosas.

La Alsacia, habiendo invadido a la Lorena, y los lorenos completamente derrotados, la guerra terminó.

Una vez terminada la sangrienta pesadilla y todo el mundo en paz, no había más que prepararse para la nueva guerra.

La repartición de medallas, condecoraciones y caramelos conmemorativos duró seis meses.

La construcción de monumentos de victoria en forma de águila, citrones, gallos, mocos, paralepípedos, sabañones, relámpagos, etc., ocupó otros seis meses. Se fijó la fecha de los aniversarios gloriosos y todo el año siguiente fue día de fiesta, todo el año se vió cruzado de cabalgatas floridas, de procesiones que giraban en torno de cada monumento. De todos los rincones del mundo venían grupos diversos a colocar como homenaje ante esos símbolos de la gloria, conejos embalsamados, coronas de cigarrillos turcos, canarios domesticados, bisteques melodiosos dentaduras de vírgenes, anafes de petróleo patinados por los siglos.

Los olivos de la paz florecían en los sombreros de todos los hombres y en las medias de todas las mujeres. Todo el mundo estaba contento y bendecía el nombre de los grandes jefes que les habían conducido a la guerra. El talón oro había caído bajo el talón de las pantuflas o babuchas o chinelas. Millones de obreros sin trabajo cantaban felices al son de sus guitarras bien comidas, a la luz de la luna. Los periódicos de los diferentes países hablaban de los encantos de la próxima guerra, insultaban al futuro enemigo que era proclamado asesino, bandido, vampiro, lamedor de

defeat. Our racial superiority is undeniable. The elegance and beauty of our women are unrivalled anywhere. The keen talent of our men, their *esprit*, how can it be compared with the nebulous and greasy intelligence of the Mammarists, an impure race with no secular traditions? Why were we defeated? What an unfathomable mystery! Why were we defeated? Was it due to the financial and artistic crisis? Was it because of the lack of regular exercise by our troops? Or was it because our soldiers had not taken an aperitif that day? The defeat is impossible to explain. It will remain a conundrum to history.

The cathedral, Hans Gunter, the City of Light, the wounded poly-glot and the Black Forest came down from the cathedral terrace. By spinning around and around, they turned into carousels; from their stomachs emerged a happy and infernal music; small sleds grew on the calluses of their feet, and hundreds of tops spun all around them. Enormous whirl-winds appeared which swallowed up the Generals Hannibal, Nelson, Moltke, Pompey, Hernán Cortés and Napoleon and transformed them into buttonhole roses.

With Alsace having invaded Lorraine, and having completely defeated the Lorrainers, the war came to an end.

Once the bloody nightmare was at an end and all the world was at peace, there was nothing else for it but to prepare for the next war.

The distribution of medals, decorations and commemorative candies lasted six months.

The construction of victory monuments in the form of eagles, lemons, roosters, snot, parallelepipeds, chilblains, lightning-bolts, etc., took another six months. The date for the glorious anniversary was set and the entire following year was one long celebration; the whole year filled with flower parades, processions revolving around each monument. From all corners of the world came various groups to lay tributes to those symbols of glory: taxidermied rabbits, wreaths of Turkish cigarettes, domesticated canaries, melodious steaks, virgins' dentures, oil-fired stoves with the patina of centuries.

Olives of peace blossomed in every man's hat and in every woman's stockings. All the world was happy and blessed the names of the great leaders who had led them to war. The gold standard had fallen under standard slippers or sandals or clogs. Millions of unemployed labourers sang happily by moonlight to the sound of their well-nourished guitars. Newspapers from a number of countries spoke of the allure of the approaching war,

cementerios, violador de selvas vírgenes y de fetos, bárbaro cavernícola, Atila, necrófilo, mutilador de gulf streams, ladrón de volcanes y de péndulos, cobarde, sembrador de pulgas intoxicadas y tantas otras cosas difíciles de anotar de paso.

Entre tanto, en las ciudades y en los campos las gentes comían deliciosas velas, cerrojos en salsa Pompadour, ensaladas de llaves ganzúas, jergones a la mayonesa, corbatas a la crema y chirridos de puerta a la Duncan. Bebían glicerina helada, el sudor de sus frentes y leche de perra terranova con tinta Parker.

En esos años maravillosos, las finanzas marchaban de mejor en mejor, como siempre después de las guerras; esto sobre todo, gracias al magnífico plan Dupont, luego mejorado por el eficaz plan Schulzl, el cual a su vez fue superado por el plan Eggg, el cual aún fue mejorado, aunque parezca imposible, por el plan del Presidente Cheese y el de la coronela Checkmate. Estos planes se ocupaban de resolver todos los problemas económicos y familiares, principalmente la compra de materias tías y materias últimas, tan necesarias a la fabricación de derivados, reemplazar el pan por ampolletas eléctricas, los pollos por virutas de espejo, las langostas por anteojos de cura.

En aquel entonces se creó la gran Sociedad de las Visiones. Era este un centro internacional de unión y de concordia un tribunal super- humano cuya sede se estableció en la punta del Tupungato. Allí se pronunciaban hermosos discursos insecticidas, mientras los miembros de la organización oían religiosamente balanceándose en sus columpios bajo los árboles atentos. Llamó mucho la atención el discurso del gran orador Pérez, sobre el arte delicado del *voyeur,* la manera de abrir un agujero en el muro de un hotel, mejor aun de una honesta casa de tolerancia y ver todo lo que pasa en el cuarto vecino. No menos espléndido fue el discurso del delegado Cook sobre los efectos insuperables de la cocaína y la morfina, muy recomendada para los octogenarios y sobre todo, en la lactancia de los nonagenarios. Pronto la Sociedad de las Visiones dedicó todas sus energías a componer dulces berceuses y canciones para las primeras comuniones.

Un día de calor, la Sociedad se diluyó completamente. Sólo quedaron en algunos asientos, pequeños pedazos de hielo que fueron empleados en la fabricación de refinados cockteles.

Poco después acaeció un hecho de suma importancia: la muerte del héroe de la Inmensa Guerra, el mariscal Duval. Su entierro fue algo

insulted the future enemy, who was proclaimed murderer, bandit, vampire, grave-licker, violator of virgin forests and fetuses, barbarian troglodyte, Attila, necrophile, mutilator of gulf-streams, thief of volcanoes and pendulums, coward, spreader of poisonous fleas and so many other things too difficult to note down in passing.

Meanwhile, in the cities and in the countryside, people ate delicious candles, latches in *Pompadour* sauce, lock-pick salads, mattresses with mayonnaise, neckties with cream and door-squeaks *à la Duncan*. They drank iced glycerine, the sweat from their browsm and Newfoundland dog's milk with Parker ink.

During those marvellous years, the financial situation got better and better, as is always the case after a war; this was above all thanks to the magnificent Dupont Plan, then improved by the effective Schulzl Plan, which in turn was surpassed by the Eggg Plan, which was improved yet again, impossible as it might seem, by the plan of President Cheese and that of Colonel Checkmate. These plans addressed the solution of all economic and domestic problems, mainly the purchase of raw-auntie materials and finished materials, so necessary for the manufacture of by-products, and for the replacement of bread with electric light-bulbs, chickens with mirror shavings, and lobsters with curate's spectacles.

At about this time the great Society of Visions was created. This was an international centre of union and mutual understanding, a superhuman court whose HQ was established on the peak of Mt. Tupungato. Fine insecticidal speeches were given there, the members of the organization listening religiously, swaying back and forth on their swings under attentive trees. A speech by the great orator Pérez – concerning the delicate art of the voyeur, the method of making a hole in a hotel wall, better still in that of an honest house of pleasure, thus to see everything happening in the next room – attracted a lot of attention. No less splendid was the speech by the delegate Cook on the unsurpassed effects of cocaine and morphine, highly recommended for octogenarians and above all, for the breastfeeding of nonagenarians. Soon the Society of Visions devoted all its energies to composing sweet lullabies and songs for first communions.

One hot day, the Society completely melted away. There only remained, on a few seats, small pieces of ice that were used in the preparation of refined cocktails.

Shortly afterwards, an event of the greatest importance occurred: the death of the hero of the Enormous War, Marshal Duval. His burial

sublime. Raras veces se había visto semejante espectáculo. Millones de
personas asistieron a sus funerales. Todas las tropas desfilaron con sus
banderas, sus trofeos y sus abuelas. El féretro del mariscal iba colocado
en la punta de un cañón. A cada cañonazo, el féretro saltaba al cielo y
volvía a caer a su sitio con una precisión maravillosa, como las pelotitas
de carey en los chorros de agua. Detrás del ataúd del gran jefe, marchaba
tristemente su caballo desnudo, el caballo que el héroe había montado
en sus grandes batallas; más atrás seguía su perro favorito, aullando a la
muerte, luego venía el gato de luto, el loro con los ojos llenos de lágrimas,
marchando al mismo paso solemne de su canario tan amado. Después
seguían sus zapatos, los últimos tres pares de zapatos que el mariscal había
puesto en sus intrépidos pies, detrás, su bastón marchaba a la altura de
la mano, su sombrero a la altura de la cabeza y el último cigarro fumado
hasta la mitad, el día antes de su muerte, marchaba afligido a la altura
de la boca. Luego, bajo un inmenso palio y llevado por cuatro reyes,
venía en un espléndido bocal de piedras preciosas la próstata del ilustre
jefe. Seguían detrás, en el orden en que les nombraremos: el cardenal en
velocípedo y diez obispos en bicicletas, la cámara y el senado en patines,
el presidente y sus ministros y luego los académicos con sus cucharas
envainadas debajo de la casaca verde limón.

En honor del mariscal y para perpetuar su memoria entre los hombres,
todas las avenidas, las plazas y las calles fueron bautizadas con su nombre.
En medio del entusiasmo general todos los ríos, las montañas, los árboles,
las flores, los animales, los insectos, fueron bautizados Duval. Todas las
familias se llamaron Duval. Dios fue honrado por los creyentes con el
nombre de Duval. Los mejores platos en los restaurantes, y los mejores
vinos, se llamaron Duval. Pronto todo se llamó. Duval. Así la lengua fue
extremadamente hermosa y simple. Cuando dos amigos se encontraban en
una calle o en un bar, se hablaban en el más puro duval. Uno decía al otro:

—Duval, duval, duvalduval, duvalval.

Lo que antes se habría dicho: Es increíble el número de cochinos
extranjeros que hay en el mundo.

El marido, al volver a casa, contaba a su mujer los acontecimientos
del día:

—Duval, duvalduvalduval, duval, duvalduval, duval, duval.

Lo que quería decir en lenguaje vulgar: esta tarde perdí un guante en
las Galeries Lafayette.

Su mujer le respondía:

was something sublime. Rarely had such a spectacle been seen. Millions of people attended his funeral. All the troops marched with their flags, their trophies and their grandmothers. The marshal's coffin was placed on the muzzle of a cannon. With each volley from the cannon, the coffin jumped into the sky and fell back into place with marvellous precision, like little tortoiseshell balls on water jets. Behind the great leader's coffin, his uncovered horse walked sadly, the horse that the hero had ridden in his great battles; further back followed his favourite dog, howling at death, then came the cat in mourning, the parrot with tears in its eyes, walking with the same solemn pace as his beloved canary. There then followed his shoes, the last three pairs of shoes that the marshal had worn on his intrepid feet; behind them his cane marched along at hand height, his hat at head height, and his last cigar, half-smoked the day before his death, marched grieving at mouth height. Then, under an immense canopy and carried by four kings, there came – in a splendid jar of precious stones – the illustrious leader's prostate. Behind all these there followed, in order: the Cardinal on a penny-farthing, ten bishops on bicycles, the Chamber and the Senate on roller-skates, the President and his ministers and then the academicians with their spoons sheathed under lime-green cloaks.

In honour of the Marshal and to perpetuate his memory amongst the population, all avenues, all squares and all streets were named after him. Amidst the general enthusiasm, all rivers, mountains, trees, flowers, animals, insects, were named Duval. All families were named Duval. God was honoured by believers with the name of Duval. The best dishes in restaurants, and the best wines, were called Duval. Soon everything was called Duval. Thus the language was extremely beautiful and simple. When two friends met on a street or in a bar, they spoke to each other in the purest Duval. One said to the other:

"Duval, duval, duvalduval, duvalval."

Or, as one would have said before: "It's incredible how many foreign pigs there are in the world."

The husband, on returning home, told his wife about the events of the day:

"Duval, duvalduvalduval, duval, duvalduval, duval, duval."

Which is to say, in the vulgar tongue: "This afternoon I lost a glove at Galeries Lafayette."

His wife answered him:

¿Duvalduval duval, davuldu val, duduval? Duval, duvalduvalduval-duval, duval, duval.

Lo que puede traducirse así en lengua inculta: ¿No sería en otra parte? Te diré que la cocinera quemó el asado. Esto te pasa por llegar tarde.

A lo cual el marido contestaba, colérico: Duval.

Queriendo decir en el viejo idioma: mierda.

"Duvalduval duval, davuldu val, duduval? Duval, duvalduvalduval-duval, duval, duval.

Which can be translated into uncouth language thus: "Couldn't it be somewhere else? I'll tell you, the cook burned the roast. That's what you get for being late."

To which the husband replied, angrily: "Duval."

Meaning in the old language: "Shit."

VICENTE HUIDOBRO

DOS EJEMPLARES DE NOVELA

POLLENZA 1932

VICENTE HUIDOBRO

TWO EXAMPLES
OF NOVELS

POLLENZA 1932

Palma de Mallorca,
agosto de 1932.

Señor Hans Arp.

Querido Hans:

Aprovechando mi estada en Barcelona, camino de Mallorca, en
donde voy a pasar mis vacaciones, llevé a un editor, nuestras *Tres novelas*
ejemplares. El editor las encontró cortas para hacer un libro y me he visto
obligado a escribir yo solo, otras dos más. Estas dos, que he titulado *Dos*
ejemplares de novela te las dedicaré a ti en recuerdo de aquellas vacaciones,
que pasamos juntos en Arcachón y de esas noches, cuando a la hora de
la sobremesa nos entreteníamos en escribir juntos las tres novelas *tan*
ejemplares que encabezan este libro. Aún tengo en los oídos tus risas y
aún me parece ver esos relámpagos repentinos que iluminaban nuestros
ojos en ciertos momentos.

Siempre creí imposible escribir un libro en colaboración con alguien y
poder acordar mis instrumentos con loo de otro. Contigo la cosa marchó
tan bien, que no me lo puedo explicar sino por cierta confraternidad
espiritual que es seguramente la razón por la cual nuestra amistad ha sido
siempre sólida y sin manchas.

Muchos dirán al leer estas páginas que nosotros sólo sabemos reír.
Ignoran lo que la risa significa, ignoran la potencia de evasión que hay
en ella. Además creen que un poeta no puede presentar varios aspectos;
tienen el alma monocorde y juzgan a los demás como son ellos.

Estas páginas no corresponden, claro está, a toda nuestra obra ni a
todo nuestro ser integral. Son sólo una faceta de nuestro espíritu y mal
nos juzgaría, quien sólo a través de ellas quisiera vernos. Sin embargo hay
en ellas algo más que risas y que burlas.

En mi pieza de teatro *Gilles de Raiz*, hay una escena en la cual Gílles
dice: "Si no riera en este instante, mi cerebro estallaría". Para cuántos
hombres la risa es una válvula de escape salvadora como lo es el llorar.
Cuantas veces habríamos estallado si no hubiéramos reído. El alma
popular que posee tantas intuiciones lo ha indicado en uno de sus dichos
más corrientes: "Estalló en carcajadas. Estalló en lágrimas". Esas frases
encierran en si un concepto más profundo que el que ellas creen poseer
y que el que las gentes le atribuyen: tan profundo que se les ha pasado

Palma de Mallorca,
August 1932.

Mr. Hans Arp.

Dear Hans:

Taking advantage of being in Barcelona, on my way to Mallorca, where I'm going to spend my holidays, I took our *Three Exemplary Novels* to a publisher. The publisher found them somewhat short for a book and so I was obliged to write two more on my own. These two, which I have titled *Two Examples of Novels* I will dedicate to you in memory of those holidays we spent together in Arcachon and of those nights, when we entertained ourselves during the post-prandial hours by writing together the three *such* exemplary novels that begin this book. I still feel your laughter in my ears and I still seem to see those sudden flashes of lightning that lit up our eyes from time to time.

I always thought it impossible to collaborate with someone else in the writing of a book, or to be able to get my instruments in tune with someone else's. With you it all went off so well, that I can only explain it as having arisen from some spiritual fellowship, which is surely the reason why our friendship has always been firm and unblemished.

Many will say when reading these pages that we know only how to laugh. They do not know what laughter means; they do not know the power of evasion that it contains. What's more, they believe that a poet cannot demonstrate different characteristics; they have one-dimensional souls and they judge others as if they were like themselves.

These pages do not correspond, of course, to all our work, nor to our entire being. They are only one facet of our spirit and those who would see us only through these stories would judge us poorly. However, there is more to them than laughter and mockery.

In my play *Gilles de Raiz*, there is a scene in which Gilles says: "If I didn't laugh right now, my brain would burst". For how many men is laughter an escape valve, like weeping. How many times would we have burst if we hadn't laughed. The popular soul, with all its intuition, has demonstrated this in that most commonplace of sayings: "He burst out laughing. He burst into tears." These phrases contain a more profound concept than they are thought to have, and which people generally

desapercibido. Ello significa que a veces estallamos en risas o en llantos para no *reventar.* Estoy cierto de que un día la ciencia podrá probar mi afirmación.

Pero ¿crees tú que vale la pena explicarse y explicar nuestras obras frente a posibles incomprensiones? Sabemos nosotros que nadie puede limitar nuestro campo y que la apreciación ajena sólo significa una piedra o una flor en medio de un continente o de un planeta. La poesía no está obligada a ser lo que ciertos señores quieren que sea o creen que es, ni lo que ellos ven en ella.

Un abrazo de tu viejo amigo que te quiere y te recuerda constantemente.

VICENTE HUIDOBRO

attribute to them: so profound that it has passed unnoticed. It means that sometimes we laugh or we weep so as not to *explode*. I am sure that one day science will be able to prove my claim.

But do you think that it's really worth the bother of explaining oneself, explaining our works in the face of possible misconceptions? We know that no one can limit our domain and that the appreciation of others means no more than a stone or a flower in the midst of a continent or a planet. Poetry is not obliged to be what certain gentlemen want it to be or believe it to be, nor to be that which they see in it.

A hug from your old friend who loves you and thinks of you always.

VICENTE HUIDOBRO

EL GATO CON BOTAS
Y
SIMBAD EL MARINO
O
BADSIM EL MARRANO

(Novela póstuma)

Colocado en la pared, siempre frente a mis ojos, tengo el mapa de Oratonia.

El país en que yo nací es sin duda uno de los países más interesantes que jamás han existido en el mundo. Es lo que se llama una gran nación.

Selvas de peso, montañas de cielo en pecho, ríos con toda la barba. Mi patria es la única patria digna de ser amada entre todas las patrias. Cuando yo veo un hombre nacido en otra patria, pienso para mis adentros: "¡cómo sufrirá de no haber nacido en mi patria! ¡Qué horrible desgracia!" No puedo dejar de compadecerlo con toda mi alma.

Mis compatriotas, es decir los otros habitantes que tienen la dicha de haber nacido en el mismo país que yo, son también los hombres más interesantes del mundo. Grandes, fornidos, de pelo verde y sin monóculo. Nacen con chaleco y a los once años les salen guantes naturales que desde entonces tienen que cortarse un poco cada diez días.

Los habitantes de mi país son todos oradores. Hay oradores cuya palabra perfuma las flores y hace madurar las frutas. Hay oradores cuya palabra enciende los cigarros; hay oradores que alcoholizan y embriagan a los cuales se va a pedir una frase de coñac o una frase de whisky o una frase de pisco y después de oírlos todos los escuchantes salen tambaleando y haciendo eses; hay oradores cuya palabra detiene los ríos, otros cuya palabra desabotona los gabanes o lustra los zapatos, etc. Pero entre todos los oradores se destaca el orador eléctrico, el que electriza, que electrifica y electrocuta. Su palabra enciende las ampolletas en las casas y los arcos voltaicos en las calles, ella hace correr todos los tranvías de la ciudad. Este no se detiene nunca de hablar. Si tal hiciera, todos se quedarían a

PUSS IN BOOTS
and
SINBAD THE SAILOR
or
BADSIN THE TAILOR

(Posthumous novel)

I always have the map of Oratonia mounted on the wall, right before my eyes.

The country where I was born is undoubtedly one of the most interesting that has ever existed in the world. It's what they call a great nation.

Dense forests, mountains sloping down from the heavens, real torrents of rivers. Of all countries, mine is the only one worthy of love. When I see a man born in another country, I think to myself, "How he will suffer for not being born in my homeland! What a terrible misfortune!" I cannot help feeling sorry for him with all my soul.

My compatriots – that is to say the other inhabitants who have the pleasure of being born in the same country as I – are also the most interesting people in the world. Tall, stocky, green-haired, lacking monocles. They are born with waistcoats and at the age of eleven they grow natural gloves that have to be trimmed every ten days thereafter.

The inhabitants of my country are all orators. There are orators whose words perfume flowers and ripen fruit. There are orators whose words light cigarettes; there are orators, treated with alcohol, who intoxicate those asking for a cognac phrase or a whisky phrase or a pisco phrase – after hearing them the listeners all come out reeling and staggering; there are orators whose words stop rivers, others whose words unbutton overcoats or shine shoes, etc. But amongst all the orators, it is the electric orator who stands out, the one who electrizes, who electrifies and electrocutes. His words power light-bulbs in homes and voltaic-arc lamps in the streets; they make all the city's trams run. This one never stops speaking. If that

obscuras, se pararían los tranvías; sería algo así cómo una huelga general. Tal acto sería un acto de sabotaje.

Al orador eléctrico se le cuida con un esmero nunca visto. Se le revisa a cada momento para que no vaya a tener tropiezo alguno ni el menor desperfecto. Cuatro obreros, que se reanudan cada tres horas, están encargados de aceitarle las mandíbulas. Se le nutre por el trasero con lavativas de sopa de albóndigas, con erizos y huevos fritos, perdices en escabeche y muchas otras exquisiteces que su trasero de gourmet paladea y sabe estimar en lo que valen.

Para el caso de una pana imprevista, se tienen mil discos con su voz; pero se ha visto, después de repetidos experimentos, que con los discos los tranvías andan mucho más despacio y las ampolletas eléctricas pierden un 53 por ciento de su energía.

Hace algunos años que vivo lejos de mi país, pero la nostalgia me hace recordar sus paisajes y su conformación como si los tuviera siempre ante los ojos. Para consolarme de la ausencia, leo y releo su historia. Recuerdo su pasado, estudio su presente y trato de adivinar su porvenir.

En Oratonia hay tres grandes partidos políticos. El partido de aquéllos a los cuales les tiembla la mano derecha al llevarse una copa a los labios y que se llama el partido de los *sanvitistas,* el partido de aquéllos a los cuales les tiembla la mano izquierda y que se llama el partido de los *espiroquetistas,* y el partido de aquéllos a los cuales les tiemblan las dos piernas y que tienen el ombligo en relieve como un escapulario, estos se llaman los *tetraomblipernalistas.* Como este nombre era un poco largo, hoy el pueblo los llama los ponchistas, porque fueron desterrados a raíz de un complot a donde el diablo perdió el poncho.

Ese complot fue algo terrible y que puso al país al borde del desastre total. Por allá por los años de Mari Aceituna, llegó a Oratonia el anarquista Juan Sabotero y empezó a tramar una conspiración contra el gobierno. Los conspiradores, todos miembros del partido ponchista, se reunían en un sótano abandonado, debajo de un galpón medio en ruinas que primero perteneció a los jesuitas, luego fue él escondite de una banda de monederos falsos, después fue un molino, cuyo dueño sé suicidó y donde penaron las ánimas varios años, y por último perteneció a los francmasones. Allí se reunían todas las noches a las doce en punto los conspiradores ponchistas. Las conspiraciones se multiplicaban y se repetían de un modo inaceptable. Los espiroquetistas estaban entonces en el poder y la policía espiroquetista corría de un lado para otro sin

occurred, everyone would be left in darkness and the trams would stop; it would be something like a general strike. Such an act would amount to sabotage.

The electric orator is cared for with a degree of conscientiousness never seen before. He is checked at every moment so that there will be no setbacks or even the slightest flaw. Four workmen, alternating every three hours, are tasked with oiling his jaws. He is fed through his rear end with enemas of meatball soup, with hedgehogs and fried eggs, pickled partridges and many other delicacies that his gourmet rear savours and the value of which it can judge.

In the event of an unforeseen breakdown, there are a thousand discs containing his voice, but it has been observed – after repeated experiments – that when the discs are used the trams go much more slowly and electric light-bulbs lose 53 percent of their energy.

For some years I have been living far away from my country, but nostalgia allows me to recall its landscape and its structure as if they were always before my eyes. To console me in my absence, I read and re-read its history. I remember its past, study its present and try to predict its future.

There are three main political parties in Oratonia: the party of those whose right hand trembles when lifting a cup to their lips, and who are called the *Saintvitusists*; the party of those whose left hand trembles, who are called the *Spirochetists*; and the party of those whose two legs tremble and whose navel is raised like a scapular; these are called the *Tetraumbilitremorists*. As this name was a little lengthy, today people call them the *Beyondists*, because they were banished to the back of beyond following one of their plots.

That plot was a terrible affair and led the country to the brink of total disaster. Back then, in times immemorial, the anarchist John Saboteur arrived in Oratonia and began to concoct a plot against the government. The conspirators, all members of the Beyondist party, gathered in an abandoned cellar, under a half-ruined shed that had originally belonged to the Jesuits; after that, it was the hideout for a band of counterfeiters; then it was a mill, whose owner committed suicide and where ghosts were seen for many years after; finally it belonged to the Freemasons. It was there that the Beyondist conspirators met every night at twelve o'clock sharp. The conspiracies multiplied and spread in an unacceptable manner. The Spirochetists were then in power and the Spirochetist police ran all over the place without being able to discover the hideout of the

poder descubrir la madriguera de los enemigos del gobierno.

El presidente había declarado rotundo: en Oratonia nadie conspira sino yo.

Un día, la audacia de Juan Sabotero pasó todos los límites y éste fué atrapado en el momento mismo en que arrojaba una piedra entre las mandíbulas del orador eléctrico. Sabotero fue cogido en flagrante delito y llevado a la cárcel entre los insultos y las amenazas de la muchedumbre que quería lincharlo. En la cárcel fue sometido a pequeñas torturas para hacerlo hablar. Se le leyeron algunos libros de autores célebres, se le dieron sandwichs de caviar, se le hizo oír cuatro misas cantadas, se le quemaron los ojos, le mutilaron la nariz, le rajaron el vientre, le cortaron la cabeza, los brazos, las piernas, luego le arrancaron la lengua, le arrojaron en una caldera de plomo derretido, le ataron a la cola de un potro salvaje, le mostraron sesenta y siete cuadros de los más famosos pintores, le hicieron oír dos conferencias, le dieron jamón con crema de fresas, etc. Al fin Juan Sabotero confesó todo, dió los nombres de sus cómplices y el sitio de las reuniones clandestinas. En premio de su traición, se le puso en libertad inmediata y se le prometió una cartera de ministro para tenerlo grato y que no conspirara más. Al salir de la cárcel, Juan Sabotero se sacudió como un perro que sale del agua y se alejó silbando calle arriba.

Esta es la historia de la famosa conspiración que costó la vida a muchos miles de ciudadanos corno el lector se habrá percatado.

Entre tanto los sanvitistas, aprovechando que los espiroquetistas estaban ocupados en sofocar a los ponchistas, asaltaron el palacio de gobierno y se tomaron el poder.

A los pocos meses de estar los sanvitistas en el poder, empezaron a complotar contra el nuevo gobierno los espiroquetistas, que no podían resignarse con su derrota. Todas las noches se reunían en el famoso sótano que había pertenecido a los jesuitas, a los monederos falsos, al molinero suicidia y penador, a la francmasonería y luego por tres meses a unos contrabandistas de cocaína.

En vano la policía sanvitista buscaba a los conspiradores entre cielo y tierra. No había modo de descubrir su escondite.

De repente estalló la revolución. Las tropas sanvitistas se batían heroicamente contra los espiroquetistas. El nuevo presidente de la república dirigía en las calles el ataque contra los revolucionarios.

Los ponchistas, aprovechando la confusión, se tomaron el palacio de gobierno y se instalaron en él. Después de tres días de batalla en las

government's enemies.

The President had declared emphatically: "In Oratonia, no-one conspires but me."

One day, John Saboteur's audacity surpassed all limits and he was caught at the very moment he was throwing a stone between the jaws of the electric orator. Saboteur was caught *in flagrante delicto* and taken to prison amid insults and threats from the crowd that wanted him lynched. In prison he was subjected to small tortures to make him talk. Some books by famous authors were read to him; he was given caviar sandwiches; he was made to sit through four sung masses; his eyes were burned, his nose mutilated, his belly slit open, his head cut off, his arms, his legs; then they ripped out his tongue, threw him into a cauldron of molten lead, tied him to the tail of a wild horse, showed him sixty-seven pictures by the most famous painters, made him listen to two lectures, gave him ham with strawberry cream, and so on. In the end John Saboteur confessed everything, gave up the names of his accomplices and the location of their clandestine meetings. As a reward for his treachery, he was immediately released and promised a ministerial portfolio in order to keep him happy, and away from further conspiracy. On leaving prison, John Saboteur shook himself like a dog coming out of the water and whistled on up the street.

This is the story of the famous conspiracy which, as the reader will have realised, cost the lives of many thousands of citizens.

Meanwhile the Saintvitusists, taking advantage of the fact that the Spirochetists were busy suppressing the Beyondists, stormed the Parliament building and seized power.

Within a few months of the Saintvitusists being in power, the Spirochetists, unable to resign themselves to their defeat, began plotting against the new government. Every night they met in the famous cellar that had once belonged to the Jesuits, to the counterfeiters, to the miller (suicide and ghost), to the Freemasons and then for three months to some cocaine smugglers.

In vain did the Saintvitusist police search heaven and earth for the conspirators. There was no way of discovering their hiding place.

Suddenly the revolution broke out. The Saintvitusist troops battled heroically against the Spirochetists. In the streets the new President of the Republic led the attack on the revolutionaries.

The Beyondists, taking advantage of the confusion, seized the Parliament building and moved in. After three days of street fighting, the

calles, cuando el presidente regresó triunfante al palacio de gobierno, se encontró con que el vencedor era el jefe del partido ponchista.

El presidente sanvitista fue apresado y condenado a cadena perpetua. Se le encadenó a las rocas del más alto picacho de la montaña. A sus piernas se ató un jaguar que debía devorarle eternamente las entrañas y digerirlas allí encima de sus narices. Así él, acosado por el hambre, debía comer esa digestión, que a su vez el jaguar tenía que volver a devorar y así eternamente hasta el fin de los siglos, como un ejemplo para la eternidad y un símbolo de la vida universal y su interminable anillo semejante a la serpiente que se muerde la cola.

Los ponchistas, una vez en el poder y temiendo nuevas conspiraciones, decidieron convertir el célebre sótano de los descontentos en un hospital para parturientas amantes de la ópera italiana. Desde entonces, las parturientas amantes de la ópera italiana van a dar a luz en el nuevo hospital. Al llegar a la puerta del hospital no se les exige ningún documento. Ellas cantan una romanza de *Aída*, de *Tosca*, de *Traviata* o de otra ópera preferida, y pasan el umbral arrogantes y prominentes como conviene a sus condiciones raciales.

Por aquellos años sobrevino en Oratonia un terrible terremoto que derribó muchas casas y agrietó las tierras. Pronto se pudo comprobar que los comunistas eran los culpables de la catástrofe. Fueron apresados algunos dirigentes en cuyas casas descubrió la policía aparatos comprometedores: aldabas, anteojos, empanadas, un termómetro, un bidet, tres latas de sardinas, un diván, una alcachofa. Ante estos misteriosos objetos desfilaron todos los expertos del país y pudieron comprobar, después de un estudio minucioso, que ellos habían sido empleados sirviéndose de la ley de los imanes, de la variación del eje de fa tierra y el grado de las mareas, para producir la catástrofe. Los comunistas fueron quemados, y a la luz de sus cuerpos ardiendo se leyeron poemas patrióticos, y se bailó la danza nacional.

La calma volvió a reinar sobre la tierra. El país era una taza de leche, una especie de desayuno en la historia del mundo. El cielo era azul, el sol se levantaba sonriendo todas las mañanas y se dirigía optimista a sus labores diarias. Las tardes eran serenas. Las golondrinas reían a carcajadas en el espacio, jugueteando como colegialas. No había tempestades pues nadie había sembrado vientos. Grandes paraguas se balanceaban en el cielo tranquilo e inútil, pues la tierra era un cielo.

Pasados los días de epopeya, el país empezó a vivir días de idilio, de égloga y de acrósticos.

President returned triumphantly to the Parliament building, only to find that the victor was the head of the Beyondist party.

The Saintvitusist president was arrested and sentenced to life imprisonment. He was chained to rocks on the highest mountain peak. Tied to his legs was a jaguar, which would devour his entrails in perpetuity and excrete them right under his nose. Thus he, beset by hunger, had to eat those excreta, which in turn the jaguar would devour again and so on and on until the end of time, an example for all eternity and a symbol of universal life, its never-ending cycle just like the snake that bites its own tail.

Once in power, the Beyondists, fearing further plots, decided to turn the famous cellar of the malcontents into a hospital for expectant mothers who loved Italian opera. Since then, expectant mothers who are lovers of Italian opera go to the new hospital to give birth. No documents are required of them when they arrive at the hospital door. They sing an aria from *Aida*, from *Tosca*, from *Traviata* or from some other opera they prefer, and pass over the threshold arrogantly or prominently, as befits their ethnic condition.

During those times, a terrible earthquake struck Oratonia, destroying many houses, and splitting open the land. It soon became clear that the Communists were to blame for the catastrophe. Some of their leaders were arrested; in their homes the police discovered compromising equipment: door-knockers, eyeglasses, pasties, a thermometer, a bidet, three tins of sardines, a divan, an artichoke. All the country's experts paraded by these mysterious objects and were able to verify, following detailed analysis, that they had been used according to the law of magnets, the variation of the earth's axis and the range of the tides, in order to cause the catastrophe. The Communists were burned, and by the light of their burning bodies patriotic poems were read, and the national dance was performed.

Peace reigned over the land again. The country was a bowl of milk, a kind of breakfast in the history of the world. The sky was blue, the sun rose smiling every morning, and went optimistically about its daily tasks. The afternoons were calm. Swallows laughed out loud in the air, playing like schoolgirls. There were no storms, for no one had sown the winds. Great umbrellas swayed in the sky, quiet and useless, for the earth was a heaven.

The days of epic having passed, the country began to live days of idyll, eclogues and acrostics.

¿Cuánto duraría la paz y la tranquilidad? Los tiempos eglógicos no son muy largos. No debemos olvidar que la epopeya celosa nunca deja de interrumpir los idilios.

Oratonia, como todo país que se respeta, tiene su religión oficial. En Oratonia se practica el culto a la mosca. Por todas partes se levantan magníficos templos a la diosa mosca. Sus altares están siempre adornados de quesos, cornisas de jalea, ramos de miel, coronas de caca fresca y escupos maduros recogidos todas las mañanas en las bocas frutales.

En todo el país está estrictamente prohibido cubrir los guisos y los comestibles con rejillas de alambre. El propietario de una carnicería, de un almacén o de un restaurante que cubre sus carnes, su mantequilla o sus quesos o sus jamones es condenado a quince años de presidio, sin más que un simple proceso verbal, y a veces hasta a la guillotina.

Cuando una mosca se para en la nariz o trota por el cráneo calvo de un circunstante, todos le miran con religioso silencio y el elegido se inclina de orgullo y de felicidad, bendiciendo al destino que le señala corno amado de la diosa.

Los santuarios a la mosca han producido una arquitectura nueva y maravillosa. Algunos de estos santuarios son famosos por sus milagros y miles de peregrinos van a ellos en romería de todos los rincones de la tierra. Los sacerdotes de la mosca visten grandes capas de chocolate, el Sumo Sacerdote lleva además una alta torta de fresas en la cabeza y las religiosas largos velos de merengue.

En los años en que la cosecha de quesos es mala, se saca a la mosca en procesión e inmediatamente brotan quesos en gran cantidad en los sembrados y en las ventanas de las casas.

Cuando en las comidas de familia se ve en un plato una mosca muerta, en el acto se encienden dos velas y el jefe de la familia coge cuidadosamente el cuerpo de la diosa y lo coloca en los labios del más pequeño de sus hijos, porque sólo el inocente es digno de comer el celeste manjar. Si en una casa no hay moscas, la casa es destruida y en su sitio se levanta otra más apta y mejor dispuesta a la voluntad divina. El propietario en cuya casa hay mayor número de moscas, es mirado con respeto por todo el mundo. Los vecinos bendicen su nombre, le saludan al pasar como a un santo y sus rivales palidecen de envidia.

¡Qué alegría para el trabajador intelectual cuando siente en torno a su cabeza el ronroneo de millones de diosas, el sagrado murmullo! El sabe que esto significa que su trabajo es agradable al cielo y que tendrá recompensa.

How long would the peace and quiet last? Eclogic times do not last for very long. We must not forget that the jealous epic never ceases to interrupt idylls.

Oratonia, like every self-respecting country, has its official religion. In Oratonia the cult of the fly is practiced. Everywhere magnificent temples are raised to the fly goddess. Their altars are always adorned with cheeses, cornices of jelly, branches of honeycomb, crowns of fresh shit, and ripe spittle collected every morning from mouths that eat fruit.

All over the country it is strictly forbidden to cover stews and other foodstuffs with wire mesh. The owner of a butcher's shop, a grocer's or a restaurant that covers its meat, butter, cheese or hams, is sentenced – after no more than a simple hearing – to fifteen years in prison, and sometimes even the guillotine.

When a fly lands on a bystander's nose, or trots across his bald skull, everyone regards him with religious silence and the chosen one bows with pride and happiness, celebrating the fate that marks him out as beloved of the goddess.

The shrines of the fly have produced wonderful new architecture. Some of these shrines are famous for their miracles, and thousands of worshippers make pilgrimages to them from all corners of the globe. Priests of the fly wear large cloaks of chocolate; the High Priest also wears a tall strawberry cake on his head, and female celebrants wear long meringue veils.

In years when the cheese harvest is bad, the fly is taken out in a procession and instantly large numbers of cheeses sprout in the fields and in the windows of houses.

At family meals, when a dead fly is seen on a plate, two candles are lit at once and the head of the family carefully takes the body of the goddess and places it between the lips of the youngest of his children, because only the innocent is worthy to eat the heavenly delicacy. If there are no flies in a house, that house is destroyed and another is built in its place, more suitable and better disposed to the divine will. The owner of the house which has the greatest number of flies is regarded with respect by everyone. Neighbours bless his name, greet him like a saint as he passes, and his rivals go pale with envy.

What joy for the intellectual worker when he feels around his head the purring of millions of goddesses, the sacred murmur! He knows this means that his work is pleasing to Heaven and that he will be rewarded.

En cambio, ¡ay de aquél en el cual nunca se para una mosca! El infeliz es acusado y entregado al tribunal de la Santa Indignación.

Allí se le somete a un largo interrogatorio y a la prueba. Se le pone una mosca en la nariz y se cuenta el tiempo. Si la diosa se vuela antes de 15 segundos, el acusado es convicto de ateo, de brujo o de prácticas satánicas, y se le condena a ser quemado vivo. Sus cenizas son arrojadas al viento.

El culto de la mosca hoy se va extendiendo por todas partes, gracias a miles de misioneros de Oratonia que parten en todas direcciones a convertir a los infieles y predicar entre los bárbaros la única religión verdadera. Los misioneros queman los ídolos falsos, construyen templos y seminarios para enseñar la buena doctrina, hacen milagros extraordinarios animados por la gracia divina. A veces estallan guerras religiosas. La culpa es siempre de algún pueblo reacio que no quiere abandonar sus viejas creencias. Felizmente la luz celeste siempre acaba por abrirse camino y triunfar. En algunas partes se ha mezclado la mosca esencial con la mosca Tse-Tsé, produciendo así una superdiosa que, nutrida con amapolas, da a los hombres un sueño limpio de símbolos sexuales, inocente y maravilloso.

El pueblo elegido ha logrado con su culto crear una raza fuerte y sana. Gracias a la mosca, en Oratonio no hay enfermedades. La estatura media de los hombres, es de dos metros cuarenta, y el término medio de la vida guarda la misma proporción: 240 años.

Como nunca ha de faltar la mala hierba y los herejes en los pueblos, tampoco podían faltar en Oratonia. Varias sectas escondidas han pretendido difundir el culto de otros dioses. ¡Cómo no recordar aquéllos imbéciles que proclamaban el culto del dios ratón! Estos fantásticos no podían dormir sin sentir trotar en el entretecho de sus casas los regimientos de sus falsos dioses. Ellos empezaron su propaganda de un modo verdaderamente inicuo. Vendían por las calles veneno contra los ratones. Luego se descubrió que el tal veneno era una pasta de queso con confituras, robados en los templos de la mosca y a la cual pasta añadían un poderoso afrodisíaco para que sus dioses se multiplicaran hasta el infinito. Felizmente estos sectarios sacrílegos fueron descubiertos y quemados vivos. Así la herejía fue sofocada al nacer.

Pero no faltaron falsos profetas que brotaron de la tierra como por encanto y empezaron a predicar de culto al piojo. Esta nueva religión tomó más cuerpo que la anterior y puso en grave peligro la existencia misma de la nación. Estallaron revoluciones, guerras civiles y religiosas,

By contrast, woe to the one on whom a fly never lands! The wretch is charged and handed over to the court of Holy Indignation.

There he is subjected to a lengthy interrogation and is tested. A fly is placed on his nose, and the passage of time measured. If the goddess flies off within 15 seconds, the accused is convicted of atheism, witchcraft or satanic practices, and is condemned to be burned alive. His ashes are thrown to the winds.

Today the cult of the fly is spreading everywhere, thanks to thousands of missionaries from Oratonia, who set off in all directions to convert the infidels and preach the one true religion amongst the barbarians. The missionaries burn false idols, build temples and seminaries to teach proper doctrine, and perform extraordinary miracles, inspired by divine grace. Sometimes religious wars break out. It is always the fault of some recalcitrant people who do not wish to abandon their old beliefs. Happily, the celestial light always ends up opening the way, and triumphing. In some places the basic fly has been crossed with the tsetse fly, thus producing a super-goddess which, fed on poppies, gives men innocent and marvellous dreams, free from any sexual symbols.

The chosen people have succeeded with their cult in creating a strong and healthy race. Thanks to the fly, there are no diseases in Oratonia. The average height of men is two metres forty, and the average life span is in the same proportion: 240 years.

Just as there is never a shortage of weeds or heretics in villages, so they could not be lacking in Oratonia either. Several secret sects have tried to spread the cults of other gods. Who can forget those imbeciles who proclaimed the cult of the mouse-god! These fantastic people could not sleep without feeling regiments of their false gods trotting through the lofts of their houses. They began their propaganda in a truly iniquitous way. They sold mouse poison in the streets. It was later discovered that this poison was a paste of cheese and jam, stolen from the temples of the fly, and to which was added a powerful aphrodisiac so that their gods would multiply infinitely. Happily these sacrilegious sectarians were discovered and burned alive. Thus was the heresy suffocated at birth.

But there was no lack of false prophets springing from the earth, as if by magic, who began to preach the cult of the louse. This new religion took on a more solid form than the old one and seriously endangered the very existence of the nation. Revolutions broke out, as did civil and

aparecieron caudillos en diferentes partes, del país. Regimientos enteros desenvainaban sus espadas en nombre de este otro falso dios.

Se diría que es imposible la tranquilidad en la tierra.

En vista del grave peligro, los tres grandes partidos históricos, los sanvitistas, los espíroquetistas y los ponchistas se unieron. Se proclamó la alianza sagrada ante el enemigo común. Luego se nombró un generalísimo con calidad de presidente y dictador, y para ayuda de éste, como su brazo derecho, se nombró también un coronelísimo.

La primera batalla duró cuatro días y diez noches. El triunfo quedó indeciso. Entonces el coronelisimo hizo matar al generalísimo y se proclamó generalísimo y dictador absoluto con calidad de cónsul, procónsul y emperador. La suerte le sonrió como sonríe a los audaces. Libró otra batalla a los rebeldes y los despedazó completamente.

La victoria fue celebrada en la capital con embanderamiento, bailes, fiestas y un gran banquete oficial en la plaza pública. El nuevo dictador, el generalísimo en persona presidía este banquete. Las bananas salían de los fruteros por sus propios pies, se pelaban con sus propias manos y de un salto se metían en la boca del gran jefe.

Sin embargo, ya hemos dicho que es imposible la tranquilidad en la tierra. Algunos de los vencidos en la última revolución, lograron escapar a la matanza general. Uno de ellos se disfrazó de sacerdote de la mosca y con el rostro cubierto por una cogulla, se escurrió entre las sombras de la noche. Saltó por una ventana y clavó su puñal traidor en medio del corazón del orador eléctrico.

Toda la ciudad quedó a obscuras, se detuvieron los tranvías y el pánico se apoderó de los espíritus más recios.

El dictador se debatía en las sombras, se estrellaba contra los muebles, se azotaba la cabeza, caía y se levantaba. Se dió orden de buscar por todas partes otro orador eléctrico, entre tanto se echaría mano a los discos. Pero el asesino misterioso había roto todos los discos.

Habría que volver por un tiempo a las bujías. Sólo por un tiempo, pues era seguro que pronto aparecería un nuevo orador eléctrico. Acaso en los funerales del gran orador se revelaría de repente el que podría substituirlo Así, pues, al día subsiguiente, toda la ciudad estaba en el cementerio para oír los discursos.

El primero en hablar fue el mismo dictador en persona. Su figura imponente, su cabeza cuadrada, sus orejas de quitasol, su nariz de bicicleta, revelaban al político de raza. Sus ojos de tintero mostraban claramente

religious wars; warlords appeared in different parts of the country. Entire regiments drew their swords in the name of this new false god.

It is said that peace on earth is impossible.

In view of the grave danger, the three great historical parties, the Saintvitusists, the Spirochetists and the Beyondists merged together. A sacred alliance was proclaimed before the common enemy. Then a Generalissimo was appointed President and dictator and, to assist him, a Colonelissimo was also appointed to be his right-hand man.

The first battle lasted four days and ten nights. Victory remained undecided. Then the Colonelissimo had the Generalissimo killed and proclaimed himself Generalissimo and absolute dictator, with the ranks of Consul, Proconsul and Emperor. Luck favoured him, as it favours the bold. He fought another battle with the rebels and completely tore them apart.

Victory was celebrated in the capital with displays of flags, dances, festivals and a grand official banquet in the main square. The new dictator, the Generalissimo himself, presided over this banquet. Bananas left the fruit bowls on their own feet, peeled themselves with their own hands and leapt into the great leader's mouth.

However, we have already said that peace on earth is impossible. Some of those defeated in the latest revolution managed to escape the general slaughter. One of them disguised himself as a priest of the fly and, face covered with a hood, he slipped through the shadows of night. He jumped through a window and plunged his traitorous dagger right into the heart of the electric orator.

The whole city remained in darkness; the trams stopped and panic seized even the most resilient spirits.

The dictator struggled in the shadows, collided with furniture, banged his head, fell over and got back up again. Orders were given to search everywhere for another electric orator; in the meantime, the discs would be used. But the mysterious assassin had smashed all the discs.

For a while they had to revert to candles. Only for a while, for it was certain that a new electric orator would soon appear. Perhaps, at the funeral of the great orator, his replacement would suddenly be revealed. So, the following day, the whole city was at the cemetery to hear the speeches.

The first to speak was the dictator himself. His imposing figure, his square head, his parasol ears, his bicycle nose – these revealed the purebred politician. His inkwell eyes clearly showed him to be a man of thought and great culture. His mouth, outlined with pencil, showed he

al hombre de pensamiento y de gran cultura. Su boca dibujada al lápiz, mostraba el hábito de escribir.

Un silencio sepulcral reinaba en torno, cuando el dictador se puso de pie. No se oía ni un suspiro, ni el vuelo de una diosa.

He aquí el discurso del dictador:

"Pueblo amado, henos aquí ante el cadáver de un hombre que no ha muerto. Tales fueron los servicios que rindió a su patria, que este cadáver está vivo. ¿Quién de vosotros no tiene aún su voz pegada en los oídos? Se me figura que lo estoy oyendo como él me oye en estos instantes solemnes. (Se oye una campana). ¿Oís esa campana? Es su voz que me responde desde la eternidad y me dice que tengo razón, que él me está escuchando complacido y que prosiga. Prosigo. Me parece, señores, que estoy sintiendo ahora mismo el aliento cálido de su voz, el aliento perfumado de sus palabras. (Se siente un perfume de flores que sube a las narices de los oyentes). ¿Sentís ese perfume de flores que nos llega en este instante? Es él, es ese cadáver que agradece mis palabras y las premia, haciéndolas realidad. (El orador que perfuma las flores, se mueve inquieto entre la multitud, se siente invadido en su terreno y levanta los ojos airados). Ese perfume me dice que prosiga, y prosigo. Este hombre que vamos a enterrar ahora aquí en la tierra, para que esté más vivo en nuestra memoria, era un hombre excepcional. Hombre de gran saber, de vasta cultura. Se me figura que le estoy oyendo. ¡Ah! sus magníficos discursos. ¡Cuánta ciencia pudimos aprender en ellos! Nunca hablaba del siglo de Epaminondas sin recordar a Pericles, ni hablaba de Aquiles sin nombrar en seguida a la justicia; cuando hablaba de Arístides, sabía recordar el ostracismo, siempre que se cortaba la cola de algún perro recordaba a Temístocles, y cuando alguno era desterrado, él no olvidaba el nombre de Alcibíades. ¡Con qué colorido su palabra mágica sabía pintarnos la batalla de Lepanto, en donde Shakespeare perdió un brazo! Y la toma de Jerusalén, en donde Milton perdió los ojos; y la retirada de los Diez mil, en donde Tasso no perdió ni un solo hombre y donde Nelson encontró gloriosa muerte con sus heroicos sicilianos. Y cuánto había viajado y visto y observado este hombre que hoy lloramos! En su juventud visitó en Roma las célebres pirámides, esas mismas pirámides, cuyos siglos contó Carlos V ante sus soldados. En Berlín visitó la tumba de Napoleón, en Chile visitó el Cerro Santa Lucia, en Notre Dame de Madrid rezó dos padrenuestros por el alma de Rómulo y Remo. Se conocía de memoria el Duomo y la Acrópolis de París y las catacumbas de Barcelona. Su

was accustomed to writing.

A sepulchral silence reigned all around when the dictator stood up. There was not a sigh to be heard, nor the flight of a goddess.

The following is the dictator's speech:

"Beloved people, we are gathered here before the corpse of a man who is not dead. Such were the services he rendered to this country, that this corpse is alive. Who amongst you does not have his voice still fixed in your ears? I imagine I hear it, as he hears me, in these solemn moments. (A bell is heard.) Do you hear that bell? That is his voice responding to me from eternity and telling me I am right, that he is pleased at what he hears me say and that I should go on. I will go on. It seems to me, gentlemen, that even now I can feel the warm breath of his voice, the perfumed breath of his words. (A floral scent rises to the nostrils of the listening public.) Do you smell that floral perfume all around us right now? It is he, that corpse, thanking me for my words and praising them, making them a reality. (The orator who perfumes the flowers moves restlessly amongst the crowd, feeling as if his territory is being invaded, and raises angry eyes.) That perfume tells me to go on, and I will go on. This man whom we are now going to bury here in the ground, so that he may be more alive in our memory, was an exceptional man. A man of great knowledge, of enormous culture. I imagine I'm listening to him. Ah, his magnificent speeches! How much science could we learn from them! He never spoke of the century of Epaminondas without remembering Pericles, nor did he speak of Achilles without mentioning justice immediately afterwards; when he spoke of Aristides, he remembered ostracism; whenever a dog's tail was cut he always recalled Themistocles; and when someone was sent into exile, he did not forget the name of Alcibiades. With what colourful magic words could he paint for us the Battle of Lepanto, where Shakespeare lost an arm! And the capture of Jerusalem, where Milton lost his eyes; and the retreat of the Ten Thousand, where Tasso did not lose a single man, and where Nelson found a glorious death with his heroic Sicilians. And how much had he travelled, seen and observed, this man whom we mourn today! In his youth he visited the famous pyramids in Rome, those same pyramids whose centuries Charles V numbered before his soldiers. In Berlin he visited Napoleon's tomb, in Chile he visited Santa Lucia Hill, in Notre Dame de Madrid he recited two Our Fathers for the souls of Romulus and Remus. He knew the Duomo, the Acropolis of Paris and the catacombs of Barcelona by heart. His description of El Greco's house, in the centre of Cairo, reflected in the

descripción de la Casa del Greco, en medio del Cairo, reflejándose en las aguas del Támesis, será inmortal. Sí, señores, todo lo que salía de labios de este hombre admirable perdurará en la memoria de sus compatriotas hasta el fin de los siglos y hasta el día de nuestro nacimiento".

Una inmensa salva de aplausos acogió las palabras del insigne dictador. Aplaudían los vivos y los muertos, aplaudían las flores y las campanas. También algunas lágrimas brillaron en muchos ojos y rodaron por la corteza de los árboles.

El ex presidente, derrocado poco ha por la tercera revolución, temblaba de envidia ante el magnífico discurso de su rival afortunado. El se creía el supremo orador de la nación, y la sublime pieza oratoria que acababa de escuchar despertaba todos sus resentimientos. Pensaba en sus adentros: pronto derrocaré a este usurpador.

La muchedumbre seguía aplaudiendo y sollozando. De cuando en cuando se oían gritos coléricos:

—Que se nos entregue el asesino.

—Queremos al asesino. El asesino. El asesino. El asesino.

El dictador, otra vez de pie, exclamó a voz en cuello de pajarita.

—Buscaremos al asesino y lo libraremos a vuestras manos justicieras. Lo buscaremos por todos los rincones del país, bajo las piedras, adentro de los árboles, detrás de las sillas. Os juro que antes de 48 meses lo habremos descubierto.

Después de esta promesa, la muchedumbre se retiró más calmada y optimista. Todos se repetían en voz baja: ayudaremos a atraparlo, todos colaboraremos en esta noble labor. Lo buscaremos bajo las piedras, sobre los árboles, detrás de las sillas, debajo de las alfombras, detrás de las nubes, bajo los puentes del viejo París, entre las piernas de los poetas y las patas de las vacas holandesas.

Pasaron los 48 meses y el asesino misterioso no aparecía por ninguna parte.

Pasaron los años, los lustros y el asesino seguía escondido en las sombras. 'Todos se miraban con recelo, todos sospechaban los unos de los otros. ¿Cómo será su cara? ¿Cómo serán sus ojos? ¿Tendrá la nariz larga o chata? ¿Será gordo o flaco, alto o bajo, rubio o moreno?

Pasaron los años y los años. Nunca se descubrió al asesino, pero un día el mar arrojó su cadáver a las playas.

waters of the Thames, will be immortal. Yes, gentlemen, everything that came from the lips of this admirable man will endure in the memory of his compatriots until the end of time, and until the day of our birth".

An immense round of applause welcomed the words of the illustrious dictator. The living and the dead applauded, the flowers and bells applauded. Also tears shone in many eyes and rolled down the bark of trees.

The former President, ousted a little before by the third revolution, trembled with envy at this magnificent speech by his fortunate rival. He believed himself to be the nation's supreme orator, and the sublime oratorical piece he had just heard awakened all his resentment. He thought to himself: "I'll soon overthrow this usurper".

The crowd kept on applauding and sobbing. From time to time angry screams could be heard:

"Hand the assassin over to us."

"We want the assassin. The assassin. The assassin. The assassin."

The dictator, on his feet again, cried out in a winged collar:

"We will search for the assassin and we will deliver him into your hands. We will search for him in every corner of the land, under stones, inside trees, behind chairs. I swear to you that we will have found him within 48 months."

After this promise the crowd withdrew, calmer and more optimistic. They all repeated *sotto voce*: "We'll help capture him; we'll all cooperate in this noble task. We'll look for him under stones, in trees, behind chairs, beneath carpets, behind clouds, under the bridges of old Paris, between the legs of poets and the hooves of Dutch cows.

48 months went by, and the mysterious killer was nowhere to be seen.

Years went by, decades, and the killer remained hidden in the shadows. Everyone watched everyone else with suspicion, each suspecting the other. What will his face be like? What will his eyes be like? Will he have a long nose, or a flat one? Will he be fat or thin, tall or short, blond- or brown-haired?

Years and years went by. The killer was never discovered, but one day the sea dumped his corpse on the beach.

LA MISIÓN DEL GANGSTER
o
LA LÁMPARA MARAVILLOSA

(Novela oriental)

La ciudad de Peterunia cambiaba de nombre según la dirección del viento. A veces se llamaba Santa Maria de los Lirios; otras veces se llamaba Kagache, otras Santarchigo, otras Philagoca, etc.

En el momento en que empieza nuestra historia, soplaba viento sudeste, y por lo tanto la ciudad se llamaba Peterunia. Para facilitar la comprensión de esta historia a nuestros amados lectores, guardaremos este nombre durante todo nuestro relato, aunque cambien los vientos cuánto les dé la gana.

Peterunia era una gran metrópoli ultramoderna, ultravioleta, ultramarina, ultramontana y ultratumbal. Era una ciudad que invitaba al estudio y a los trabajos del espíritu. Centenares de trenes, miles de tranvías, millones de automóviles, trillones de motocicletas cruzaban sus calles, sus plazas y sus avenidas, pasaban por encima de vuestras narices, por debajo de vuestras piernas, entraban por un oído y salían por el otro — con un poco de cerilla si los oídos no habían sido deshollinados en el mes, corriendo, saltando y devorando las distancias como un antropófago se devora a un misionero bien condimentado o al natural.

La ciudad de Peterunia y todo el país del cual ella era la gran metrópoli, constituía un centro intelectual y comercial de primer orden en el mundo y una de las más altas avanzadas del progreso en este siglo del progreso.

En el instante preciso en que empieza nuestra historia, la ciudad florecía como nunca. Toda clase de flores y de plantas nacían y crecían en su seno fecundo: las rosas de la poesía, las margaritas de la astronomía, los claveles de la filosofía, los crisantemos del comercio, las azucenas de la bolsa y de la banca, los nomeolvides de las compañías de seguros, los pensamientos de las compañías anónimas, las orquídeas de la química, los miosotis de la música se deshojaban en todas las esquinas y las violetas de la pintura se escondían humildes entre la hierba, etc., sin olvidar por cierto un gran número de plantas eléctricas y plantas de ataúdes u otros comestibles. El progreso es algo que nunca elogiaremos suficientemente.

THE GANGSTER'S MISSION
or
THE MAGIC LAMP

(Oriental novel)

The city of Peterunia always changed its name according to the way the wind was blowing. Sometimes it was called Saint Mary of the Lilies; at other times it was called Kagachi, other times Santarchigo, other times Philagossa, etc.

When our story begins, the wind was a south-easterly, and therefore the city was called Peterunia. To make it easier for our beloved readers to understand this story, we will retain this name throughout the tale, although the winds change whenever they please.

Peterunia was a great metropolis, ultramodern, ultraviolet, ultramarine, ultramontane and ultrasepulchral. It was a city that invited study and works of the spirit. Hundreds of trains, thousands of trams, millions of cars, trillions of motorcycles crossed its streets, its squares and its avenues, passed above your nose, under your legs, entered through one ear and left through the other – together with a little wax, if the ears had not been syringed that month – running, jumping and devouring distances as a cannibal devours a missionary, well-seasoned or raw.

The city of Peterunia and the entire country of which it was the great metropolis, constituted one of the world's leading intellectual and commercial centres, and one of the most highly advanced cities in this century of advances.

At the precise moment when our story begins, the city was flourishing as never before. All kinds of flowers and plants sprang up and grew in its fecund bosom: the roses of poetry, the daisies of astronomy, the carnations of philosophy, the chrysanthemums of commerce, the lilies of the stock exchange and of banking, forget-me-nots of insurance companies, pansies of limited companies, orchids of chemistry, myosotis of music shed their leaves in every corner and violets of painting huddled humbly in the grass, etc., not to forget a large number of power plants and plants for coffins or other foodstuffs. Progress is something we can never praise enough.

Así, pues, en el instante preciso en que empieza esta historia tan triste cuanto verdadera, los honrados comerciantes Cook y Pérez, se encontraban en su tienda, detrás de un mostrador, verificando en dos grandes libros las ganancias de la semana. Caía la tarde. La gran tienda Cook y Pérez, que no había podido evitar la caída de la tarde, había cerrado sus puertas. De pronto se oyó un ruido extraño en el hall central de la tienda, y los señores Cook y Pérez, al levantar la cabeza de sus libros, vieron consternados que un hombre con dos piernas, con dos brazos, con dos ojos, con dos orejas, con una nariz y una boca y un pecho y un vientre, venía deslizándose a la velocidad de la luz por la cadena que sostenía el gran lustro en el medio del hall. Ambos quedaron petrificados de terror. El hombre, o mejor dicho el bandido, pues semejante hombre, tal como le hemos descrito, no podía ser sino un bandido, al llegar al término de su feliz viaje quedó montado a caballo en el magnífico lustro o lámpara central a una altura de unos tres metros sobre la cabeza de los petrificados. Allí, de un modo automático, es decir absolutamente natural, dos pistolas aparecieron en la punta de sus manos y al mismo tiempo una voz acariciadora murmuraba:

—¡Arriba las manos! ¡Ay del que se mueva un pelo o pestañee o estornude siquiera! Yo soy Aladino y ésta es la Lámpara Maravillosa.

El señor Cook y el señor Pérez levantaron las manos al aire tan alto, que algunas alondras vinieron a descansar en ellas de sus largos vuelos y hasta pensaron en anidar entre sus dedos.

El hombre del lustro descabalgó de un salto, apuntando siempre sus pistolas a la cabeza de los dos honrados comerciantes.

—Amigos míos— exclamó—, yo soy Aladino o sea el gangster John Chicago, y vengo por vuestro dinero, pues no es conveniente que los hombres acumulen demasiados billetes en su poder; esto les pone pesados gruesos y melancólicos.

Sin decir más, John Chicago saludó a los señores Cook y Pérez y se dirigió a la caja de caudales. Apenas la hubo vaciado dijo adiós a sus nuevos amigos y se alejó por el camino recorrido.

—Dentro de dos minutos, pueden ustedes colocar sus brazos en su posición natural, a menos que esta os haya gustado más.

Nos parece inútil decir que al día siguiente todos los diarios de Peterunia hablaban de la proeza de John Chicago y comentaban el aparecimiento de una nueva especie animal: el gangster. El gangster era el mamífero más interesante que se había conocido. El gangster era el sueño dorado de todos los jóvenes estudiantes, de las bellas dactilógrafas y de las madres de familia.

So, at the precise moment when this sad, but true story begins the honest merchants Cook and Pérez were in their shop, behind a counter, checking the week's earnings in two large books. Night fell. The department store, Cook and Pérez, which had not been able to avoid nightfall, had closed its doors. Suddenly there was a strange noise in the store's central lobby, and when Messrs. Cook and Pérez raised their heads from the books, they were dismayed to see that a man with two legs, two arms, two eyes, two ears, a nose, a mouth, a chest and a stomach, was sliding at the speed of light down the chain that supported the great chandelier in the centre of the lobby. Both were petrified with terror. The man, or rather the bandit – for such a man, as we have described him, could not be anything but a bandit – when he reached the end of his happy journey, was mounted astride the magnificent chandelier, or central lamp, at a height roughly three metres above the heads of the petrified men. Two pistols appeared in his hands and at the same time a caressing voice murmured:

"Hands up! Beware, whoever moves a hair or blinks or even sneezes! I am Aladdin, and this is the Magic Lamp."

Mr. Cook and Mr. Pérez raised their hands so high in the air, that some larks came and perched on them after a long flight and even considered nesting between their fingers.

The man on the chandelier dismounted with a leap, still pointing his pistols at the heads of the two honest merchants.

"My friends," he exclaimed, "I am Aladdin or, that is to say, the gangster John Chicago, and I've come for your money, because it's not right for men to accumulate too many banknotes; it makes them heavy, coarse and melancholy."

Without another word, John Chicago waved to Messrs. Cook and Pérez and headed towards the safe. As soon as he had emptied it, he said goodbye to his new friends and disappeared the way he had come in.

"In two minutes, you can put your arms back in their natural positions, unless you prefer to keep them that way."

It seems pointless to relate that the next day all of Peterunia's newspapers spoke of John Chicago's feat and commented on the appearance of a new animal species: the gangster. The gangster was the most interesting mammal ever known. The gangster was the golden dream of all young students, of beautiful typists and of housewives.

Cinco días después, el millonario y distinguido banquero Terry Fox, cabeceaba en su oficina, haciendo la digestión de algunas perdices en crepe de chine y algunas langostas platinadas, cuando una sombra irreal con dos pistolas reales en cada mano apareció de pie ante él.

—Yo soy el gangster Cara de Col. ¡Arriba las manos! Me firma usted un cheque por cien mil dólares o llamo a las pompas fúnebres.

Aún no había alcanzado el millonario Terry Fox a terminar su firma, cuando el gangster Cara de Col desaparecía con el cheque en su bolsillo.

Cinco días después, la ilustre bailarina Sarahh Sahara daba un baile en su palacio a la florinata del país en donde tantos triunfos y tantos agasajos había recibido. Toda la aristocracia de la sangre y del dinero se hallaba reunida en esa magnífica fiesta.

Míster Jupirs Atlantius en persona estaba allí presente y probaba a sus amigos que él era descendiente directo de Júpiter III, último rey de la Atlántida.

Madame Joan Papis, demostraba que ella descendía de la Papisa Juana.

La señora Sardine Jonas demostraba que ella perteneció a la ilustre familia de los Amieux Frères, que, como todo el mundo sabe, fue engendrada por Jonás en el vientre de una sardina, pues la ballena le había quedado algo grande.

El gran industrial señor Soda había hecho su inmensa fortuna con su invento de la Soda Fountain, la Soda Crema y el Ice Cream Soda, tan necesarios para los motores gastados y sin duda alguna los mejores lubricantes para las hostias, las ruedas de molino, las vejigas y las linternas.

En lo mejor de la fiesta, cuando las parejas se entregaban en brazos del one step, y las señoras lucían sus collares de lámparas y los hombres sus corbatas de canapé, diez sombras aparecieron en medio del gran salón, diez sombras siniestras con diez pistolas en cada mano. El baile se detuvo como por encanto. Una voz tronó detrás de las más altas cordilleras:

—¡Arriba las manos! Buena cosecha tenemos. Gracias, San Isidro, labrador.

Las diez sombras fueron descolgando de los pechos de las damas los collares, los pendantif, los bajorrelieves, los cuadros célebres, las panoplias antiguas, etcétera.

Terminada la tarea, una mano escribió en la pared las siguientes palabras:

"John Chicago y sus discípulos el Cara de Col, el Bigotes, el Ombligo

Five days later, the distinguished banker and millionaire Terry Fox was dozing in his office, digesting some partridges in *crêpe-de-chine* and a few platinum-plated lobsters, when an unreal shadow with two real guns, one in each hand, appeared standing before him.

"I'm the gangster Cabbage Face. Hands up! You'll write me a cheque for a hundred thousand dollars, or I'll call the undertakers."

Millionaire Terry Fox had barely reached the end of his signature, when the gangster Cabbage Face disappeared with the cheque in his pocket.

Five days later, the illustrious ballerina Sarahh Sahara gave a ball in her palace for the flower of the country, in which she had experienced so many triumphs and such hospitality. All the aristocracy, of blood and of money, were gathered at that magnificent gathering.

Mister Jupirs Atlantius was there in person and proved to his friends that he was a direct descendant of Jupiter III, the last King of Atlantis.

Madame Joan Pope established that she was descended from Pope Joan.

Mrs. Sardine Jonah established that she belonged to the illustrious family of John West which, as everyone knows, was begotten by Jonah in the belly of a sardine, because the whale had been somewhat too large for him.

The great industrialist Mr. Soda had made his immense fortune from the invention of the Soda Fountain, Cream Soda and Ice Cream Soda, so necessary for worn engines and undoubtedly the best lubricants for hosts, mill-wheels, bladders and flashlights.

During the best part of the feast, when couples were busy with the one-step, and ladies wore their necklaces of lanterns and men their canapé ties, ten shadows appeared in the middle of the great ballroom, ten sinister shadows with ten pistols in their hands. The dancing stopped as if by magic. A voice thundered from beyond the highest mountain ranges:

"Hands up! A good harvest we have here. Thank you, Saint Isidore the Farmer."

From the ladies' breasts the ten shadows unhooked necklaces, pendants, bas-reliefs, famous paintings, ancient panoplies, etcetera.

Once the task was finished, a hand wrote the following words on the wall:

"John Chicago and his disciples, Cabbage Face, Whiskers, The Smiling

sonriente, Míster Cook y hermanos, el señor Pérez e hijos, saludarnos a la
ilustre concurrencia y les deseamos un feliz año nuevo".

Un minuto después, la dueña de casa salía de adentro de su reloj
pulsera, donde se había escondido, y pedía mil perdones a sus invitados
por el asalto de que habían sido víctimas en su propia casa. Entonces el
gran novelista Monsieur Woodrow Hindenburg, dijo a los asistentes:

—Señores, todo esto es la culpa del infame John Chicago, que
ha hecho escuela. Nuestro deber es combatir a ese pernicioso y a sus
discípulos por todos nuestros medios.

La señorita Joan Papis, saltando sobre una silla clamó en el desierto:

—No, señores, yo pienso que debemos seguir el ejemplo de ese ilustre
John, estudiar profundamente el gangsterismo irradiante y tratar de ser
sus mejores discípulos. Vean ustedes, cómo los señores Cook y Pérez, los
más avisados comerciantes de este país, se han hecho gangsters con todos
los miembros de sus familias.

Varias voces tronaron a la vez:

—¡Bravo! Tiene razón. Viva Joan Papis. Viva John Chícago.

A la salida del baile de Sarahh Sahara, todos sus invitados, todos
aquéllos que tenían múltiples y variados oficios, ya no tenían sino uno:
todos eran gangsters. Sólo Sarahh Sahara se resistía a cambiar de oficio.

Cinco días después, la gran Sahara, al volver una noche a su casa, se
encontraba con que su madre había sido raptada. Un papel clavado en la
silla de ruedas de la anciana, exigía la suma de sesenta mil dólares por el
rescate. El precio era elevado, sin duda alguna, dado el uso de la señora,
cuyas válvulas de escape y cuyos órganos propulsores estaban en muy mal
estado Pero la ilustre Sarahh no podía discutir ni regatear tratándose de
su madre. Pagó, y su madre le fue restituida por carta certificada.

Entonces la gran bailarina pensó que la mejor manera de rehacerse
pronto de los sesenta mil rublos perdidos era convertirse ella misma en
gangster, y así lo hizo.

El número de los gangsters aumentaba de un modo alarmante.
Había batallas en todas las esquinas de la ciudad. Pasaban y repasaban los
entierros como carruseles. Los honrados ciudadanos de Peterunia ya no
sabían qué hacer ni a quién pedir protección. Centenares de policías habían
abandonado su oficio equívoco y pasado al gangsterismo. Y no sólo policías
sino aun varios jefes, prefectos, sargentos y otros distinguidos graduados
amén de varios ilustres políticos, ministros, senadores, futbolistas, coroneles,
comandantes, manicuras y bomberos.

Navel, Mr. Cook and brothers, Sr. Pérez and sons, offer their greetings to this illustrious gathering and wish them a happy new year."

A moment later, the owner of the house emerged from inside her wristwatch, where she had been hiding, and begged a thousand pardons of her guests for the assault they had suffered in her own home. Then the great novelist Mr. Woodrow Hindenburg said to the audience:

"Gentlemen, this is all the fault of the infamous John Chicago, who has set a precedent. It is our duty to fight that pernicious man and his disciples by any and all means."

Miss Joan Pope, jumping onto a chair, cried out in the desert:

"No, gentlemen, I think we should follow the example of this illustrious John, make a thorough study of this radiant gangsterism, and try to become his best disciples. See how Messrs. Cook and Pérez, the most knowledgeable merchants in the country, have turned into gangsters, together with all their family members."

Several voices thundered out at once:

"Bravo! She's right. Long live Joan Pope. Long live John Chicago."

On leaving Sarahh Sahara's ball, all her guests, who had been employed in many and various trades, no longer had any trade but one: they were all gangsters. Only Sarahh Sahara was reluctant to change profession.

Five days later the great Sahara, returning home for the night, found that her mother had been kidnapped. A piece of paper stuck in the old woman's wheelchair demanded a ransom of sixty thousand dollars. The price was high, no doubt, given the lady's condition: her exhaust valves and organs of propulsion were in a very poor state. But the illustrious Sarahh could not argue, or haggle, when it came to her mother. She paid up, and her mother was returned by registered mail.

Then the great ballerina thought that the best way to get over the loss of sixty thousand roubles was to become a gangster herself, and so she did.

The number of gangsters increased alarmingly. There were battles in every corner of the city. Funeral processions went by again and again, coming round like carousels. The honest citizens of Peterunia no longer knew what to do or where to seek protection. Hundreds of policemen had abandoned their misguided trade and moved on to gangsterism. And not only policemen, but also several managers, prefects, sergeants and other distinguished graduates as well as a number of illustrious politicians, ministers, senators, footballers, colonels, commanders, manicurists and firefighters.

Cinco días después, el joyero Jacobo Jacobson, veía aparecer ante él la sombra trágica con la elegante pistola en la mano. Una voz de ultratumba susurraba sus oídos:

—¡Arriba las manos! Aquí todas tus joyas. Jacobo Jacobson, al ver alejarse la sombra con sus tesoros y el sudor de su frente, gritó desesperado:

—Bueno. Yo también me hago gangster.

Cinco días después, el reverendo Poison oraba en su capilla y repasaba sus proyectos y sus buenas intenciones.

Eran las 6:15 de la tarde. A las 6:30 apareció ante sus ojos meditativos la elegante pistola y la sombra trágica.

Al sentir en sus sienes el suave calor de la pistola, el reverendo levantó las manos al cielo y exclamó:

—¡My God!

La voz de la sombra irrumpió en las sombras:

—No My God. My John… my John, ¿entiende usted? My John.

Y la sombra se alejó llevándose todas las oraciones, los proyectos y las buenas intenciones del reverendo Poison, que cayendo de rodillas dijo como herido por la luz de la divina gracia:

—A partir de este momento me hago gangster.

Cinco días después se verificaba la gran reunión anual de la Academia de Ciencias de Peterunia, la sala estaba repleta de oyentes y admiradores de las bellas ciencias. El eminente sabio don Looping the Loop acababa de ser presentado a la asamblea por la célebre pintora doña Pablo y Virginia. Don Looping tenia la palabra. Sin duda alguna, el ilustre sabio era un hombre de genio, pues poseía una larga paciencia. Su paciencia, medida por el Club Internacional de Turismo, pasaba de 930 kilómetros y podía ser recorrida por un buen automóvil en un mínimo de 6 horas y 40 minutos.

El eminente sabio poseía además una bella calva que brillaba más coqueta que el diamante azul del Sultán Rojo. ¡Qué hermosa cabeza la del ilustre sabio! Sin un solo cabello y llena de azúcar flor como la telegrafía sin hilos que hace nuestros encantos en las tardes de otoño.

Nadie perdía una palabra de sus labios de coral, no volaba una mosca o si volaba, nadie oía el ruido desesperante de su motor mal aceitado. Todos los hombres de ciencia de los catorce continentes se habían dado cita en aquel congreso de eminencias. El ilustre sabio seguía desarrollando ante los ojos atónitos y los oídos ávidos la larga lista de sus descubrimientos.

Five days later, the jeweller Jacob Jacobson saw the tragic shadow appear before him, an elegant pistol in its hand. A voice from beyond the grave whispered in his ear:

"Hands up! Let's have all your jewellery." Jacob Jacobson, seeing the shadow vanish with his treasures and the sweat of his brow, shouted desperately:

"Fine, I'm going to be a gangster too."

Five days later, Reverend Poison was praying in his chapel and reviewing his projects and his good intentions.

It was 6:15 p.m. At 6:30 the elegant pistol and the tragic shadow appeared before his meditative eyes.

Upon feeling the gentle heat of the gun at his temple, the Reverend raised his hands to Heaven and exclaimed:

"Mon Dieu!"

The voice of the shadow burst into the shadows:

"Not Mon Dieu. Mon John... mon John, you understand? Mon John."

And the shadow went away, taking with him all of Reverend Poison's prayers, plans and good intentions. Falling to his knees, as if wounded by the light of divine grace, he said:

"From this moment on, I'm going to be a gangster."

Five days later the great annual meeting of the Peterunia Academy of Sciences took place. The room was filled with listeners and admirers of the fine sciences. The eminent sage Sir Looping the Loop had just been introduced to the assembly by the famous painter Lady Paul and Virginia. Sir Looping had the floor. Without a doubt, the illustrious scholar was a man of genius, for he possessed great patience. His patience, as measured by the International Touring Club, exceeded 930 kilometres in length and could be travelled by a good car in a minimum of 6 hours and 40 minutes.

The eminent scholar also possessed a beautiful bald head which shone more flirtatiously than the blue diamond of the Red Sultan. What a fine head the illustrious scholar had! Without a single hair and full of icing sugar – like the wireless telegraph that thrills us on autumn evenings.

No one missed a word that passed his coral lips, no insect flew or, if it flew, no one heard the desperate noise of its poorly oiled engine. All the scientists from the fourteen continents had gathered at that congress of eminences. The illustrious scholar continued to elaborate the long list of his discoveries before their stunned eyes and avid ears.

"Asi pues, señores, he descubierto y clasificado numerosos insectívoros y animalúnculos, entre los cuales se destacan los pertenecientes a la familia de los Sombrerífagos, los Edredónicos y los Perlípedos. He descubierto el Spirunga Phallis, que como su nombre indica, me será mejor describir en una asamblea de caballeros solos. He descubierto la Padrágora, pequeño animalúnculo cuyo origen es bastante curioso y que ya había sido previsto por ciertos sabios desconocidos. Nace la Padrágora de una gota diamantífera o perlífera que rueda por las piernas de una mujer guillotinada en el momento de caer su cabeza por haber devorado a su hijo recién nacido. La gota diamantífera o perlífera debe encontrar al llegar al suelo una pastilla de Bouillon Kub. Al contacto de la gota con el Bouillon Kub, nace la Padrágora, que es el más bello y gracioso animalúnculo que pueda soñarse. Apenas nacido, este pequeño gnomo o duendecillo, hace muzarañas con las manos y los brazos. Hace ese gesto que consiste en levantar una mano con los dedos hacia arriba, dejando un gran cóncavo al centro, gesto que significa un terrible insulto en los países de la costa del Pacífico. Corre entre las piernas de las mujeres, trepa por ellas como mono y les hace cosquillas en salva sea la parte o en sálvese quién pueda. Escribe *culo* en las paredes, y todas esas frases misteriosas que aparecen de vez en cuando en los muros de las casas; y él es el que dibuja obscenidades en la almohada de los canónigos y de los notarios. Tiene la cabeza oblonga, los ojos en pirámide y el epigastrio en arabescos de una sensibilidad extrema.

También he descubierto, señores, el Cuarentífero, el único pájaro que puede volar cuarenta días y cuarenta noches sin descanso. El único pájaro que no tiene olor a encerrado, pues sólo él no estuvo en el Arca de Noé.

Ultimamente, señores, he descubierto el Hongo Antirítmico, que es el causante del cáncer. Este Hongo que se multiplica de pronto en nuestra sangre, tiene un ritmo contrario al de nuestras células básicas. He ahí el origen del cáncer. Al multiplicarse va obligando a las células vencidas a cambiar de ritmo, y entonces, se produce el horrible mal.

También he descubierto la Pompícula, hermoso semimamífero que, como su nombre indica, bebe el agua por el ojo del trasero. Se sienta en el agua y luego bombea o pompea con el ano, valiéndose de ciertos movimientos especiales de contracción y relajación de cinco subdivisiones del esfínter...

—¡Arriba las manos!— tronó una voz en medio de la sala, y al instante cuarenta sombras alzaron cuarenta pistolas.

"So, gentlemen, I have discovered and classified numerous insectivores and animalunculi. Amongst those which stand out are those belonging to the family of the Hateaters, the Eiderdownics and the Pearlipeds. I have discovered the Spirunga Phallis which, as its name suggests, it would be better for me to describe in an assembly of gentlemen alone. I have discovered the Padragora, a tiny animalunculus whose origin is quite curious and which had already been foretold by a few unknown scholars. The Padragora is born from a diamond, or pearl droplet that rolls between the legs of a woman guillotined for having devoured her newborn son, and at the exact moment her head falls. The diamond, or pearl droplet must locate a Maggi bouillon cube when it reaches the ground. When the bead fuses with the bouillon cube, the Padragora is born... which is the most beautiful and graceful animalunculus that can be dreamed of. As soon as it is born, this little gnome, or elf, makes odd gestures with its arms and hands. It makes this gesture which consists of raising a hand with the fingers upwards, leaving a large hollow in the centre – a gesture which is a terrible insult in the countries of the Pacific coast. It runs between women's legs, climbs up them like a monkey, and tickles them you know where or who knows where. It writes *arsehole* on walls, and all those mysterious phrases that appear from time to time on the walls of houses; and it's also the one that makes obscene drawings on the pillows of clergymen and notaries. It has an oblong head, the eyes are pyramidal, and the epigastrium is arabesque and extremely sensitive.

I have also discovered, gentlemen, the Fortyer, the only bird that can fly for forty days and forty nights without rest. The only bird that has no whiff of confinement, because it's the only one that wasn't in Noah's Ark.

Most recently, gentlemen, I have discovered the anti-rhythmic mushroom, which is the cause of cancer. This mushroom, which suddenly multiplies in our blood, has a rhythm contrary to that of our base cells. That is the origin of cancer. As it multiplies, it forces the defeated cells to change rhythm, and thus produces the horrible illness.

I have also discovered the Pumpanalicule, a beautiful half-mammal that, as its name might suggest, drinks water through the hole in its behind. It sits in the water and then pumps with its anus, using certain special contracting and relaxing movements of the five subdivisions of its sphincter...

"Hands up!" thundered a voice in the middle of the room, and at once forty shadows raised forty pistols.

Un olor a escencia de rosas se esparció por el gran salón de la Academia.

Era un espectáculo hermoso el ver una gran asamblea de sabios y cerebros escogidos, con las manos levantadas al espacio como esperando la bajada de un ángel o la ruptura de la bóveda celeste.

Las cuarenta sombras hicieron un registro completo en el cuerpo de la docta asamblea, llevándose toda su ciencia, numerosas ideas nuevas y viejas, algunos grandes problemas y algunas carteras y hasta la rica gama de colores de la ilustre pintora doña Pablo y Virginia. ¡Cómo lloraba la ilustre pintora, viendo alejarse en manos extrañas sus colores y sus calores, sus corolas y sus corales!

Entonces fue cuando la docta asamblea, acordó, por una inmensa mayoría de votos, dedicarse por entero al grato oficio del gangsterismo, pensando acaso que ese era el único medio de recuperar su ciencia, sus ideas, sus ensayos, sus descubrimientos y sus esfuerzos. No debemos olvidar que la Academia es una señora anciana respetable, sorda y ciega, pero no muda y que su elocuente discurso tenía que convencer a los demás miembros de su cuerpo gentil. Así se explica la decisión tornada por la gran mayoría.

El número de los gangsters se había multiplicado de un modo increíble. Casi toda la población del país había tomado ya el interesante y lucrativo oficio. Sólo algunos recalcitrantes o cerebros atrasados no querían aún abandonar sus viejas costumbres y se resistían a entrar por el nuevo camino del bienestar y del progreso.

Los señores gangsters vivían en magníficos palacios, poseían los mejores automóviles, los mejores, yates, las mejores mujeres, los mejores hijos y los mejores padres. Comían la mejor comida, bebían la mejor bebida. Y sobre todo manejaban las finanzas y la alta política del país.

En la ciudad de Peterunia, el ochenta por ciento de los habitantes eran gangsters y se habían levantado varios monumentos al gran John. Y no sólo Peterunia, sino todas las ciudades del país ostentaban orgullosas por lo menos una estatua del insigne inventor del gangsterismo irradiante.

Se escribían libros sobre el gran John, se imprimían discos con su voz para conservarla a las generaciones venideras, se encerraba su olor en pequeñas cajitas de ónix, para tenerle siempre presente por todos los sentidos. Se le fotografiaba y se le filmaba en todas las posturas y a todas las horas del día y dé la noche.

Así se explica la desesperación general de las multitudes el día de su muerte. El ataúd del gran John se deslizaba sobre un río de lágrimas sin necesidad de apelar al remo ni a la hélice ni a las velas. El ataúd del

A scent of essence of roses wafted across the great hall of the Academy.

It was a beautiful spectacle to see a great assembly of chosen scholars and minds, hands raised to the sky as if awaiting the descent of an angel or the rupture of the celestial vault.

The forty shadows made a complete survey of the learned assembly, taking with them all its science, numerous new and old ideas, some great problems and some wallets, and even the rich range of colours used by the illustrious painter Lady Paul and Virginia. How the illustrious painter wept, seeing her colours and her calories, her corollas and her corals taken away in the hands of strangers!

It was then that the learned assembly voted, by an enormous majority, to devote themselves entirely to the pleasant task of gangsterism, thinking perhaps that this was the only means of recovering their science, their ideas, their essays, their discoveries and their endeavours. We should not forget that the Academy is a respectable old lady, deaf and blind, but not dumb, and that her eloquent speech had to convince the other members of her gracious body. This explains the decision made by the great majority.

The number of gangsters multiplied incredibly. Almost the entire population of the country had already taken to the interesting and lucrative trade. Only a few recalcitrant or backward minds did not yet wish to abandon their old ways, and were reluctant to enter the new path to welfare and progress.

The gentlemen gangsters lived in magnificent palaces, possessed the best cars, the best yachts, the best women, the best children and the best parents. They ate the best food, drank the best drinks. And above all, they handled the country's finances and high politics.

In the city of Peterunia, eighty percent of the inhabitants were gangsters and several monuments to the great John had been erected. And not just Peterunia, but every city in the country proudly displayed at least one statue of the illustrious inventor of radiant gangsterism.

Books were written about the great John, recordings of his voice were put on discs in order to preserve it for future generations; his scent was enclosed in little onyx boxes in order to ensure he was always present for all the senses. He was photographed and filmed in all postures and at all hours of the day and night.

This will explain the general despair of the crowds on the day of his death. The coffin of the great John slid on a river of tears without

ilustre inventor era de oro, construido con todos los relojes que había conquistado en su brillante carrera artística y social. El ataúd hecho de relojes y con todos los relojes andando, parecía dar vida y palpitación eterna al amado despojo que dormía el último sueño.

Y entonces se produjo el milagro. Los últimos recalcitrantes se pasaron al partido del muerto, que, como el Cid, ganó su mejor batalla en estado de cadáver. Todo el mundo abrazó la nueva religión.

Una vez que todos los habitantes de Peterunia fueron gangsters, se acabaron los gangsters en Peterunia.

FIN

any need of oars, propellers or sails. The illustrious inventor's coffin was made of gold, built with all the watches he had seized in his brilliant artistic and social career. The coffin made of watches – and with all the watches working – seemed to give life and an eternal pulse to the beloved plunderer who slept the final sleep.

And then the miracle occurred. The final recalcitrants came over to join the dead man who, like El Cid, won his finest battle as a corpse. Everyone embraced the new religion.

Once all the inhabitants of Peterunia were gangsters, there were no more gangsters in Peterunia.

END

GLOSSARY

These notes provide background to some of the names mentioned in the text.

p. 18/19 *Allons enfants de la patrie* — opening words of *La Marseillaise*, the French national anthem.

p. 28/29 *Racine, Corneille and Molière* — French dramatists of the 17th century.

Félix Potin — Potin (1820–1871) was the founder of one of the earliest mass-market retailers of own-brand goods in France. In the 1920s the chain had over 70 branches and some of the Parisian branches were in specially designed buildings.

Woolworth — I have opted for Woolworth as an Anglo-American period equivalent for Félix Potin that might still be a recognisable name.

p. 28 *Dépôt Nicolas* — I assume this is to be the still-existing wine store on Paris's Île St-Louis.

carbonarios / Carbonari — an informal network of revolutionary secret societies active in Italy in the early 19th century.

p. 30 *"un violín … célebre pintor Ingres"* — refers to a surrealist photograph by Man Ray, *Le Violon d'Ingres* (Ingres' Violin), in which a naked woman is seen from behind, seated, with two f-holes drawn on her back, as on a violin or a cello.

rue de Saussais — location of the French national police headquarters.

Austerlitz — one of the most significant battles (1805) of the Napoleonic Wars, in which the French defeated the allied Russian/Austrian/Prussian forces.

Schiller — Friedrich Schiller, German poet and dramatist (1759–1805).

p. 32/33 *Lloyd George and Woodrow Wilson* — respectively, Prime Minister of the United Kingdom (1916–1922), and President of the United States (1913–1921).

Louis XV — King of France, 1722–1774.

Cardinal Pitelli — this is probably a misprint for Cardinal P̲i̲r̲e̲l̲l̲i̲, the hero of Ronald Firbank's 1926 novel, *Concerning the Eccentricities of Cardinal Pirelli*.

p. 34/35 *King Dagobert* — There were three kings of this name, all Merovingians. Dagobert I was the king of Austrasia (623–634), king of all the Franks (629–634), and king of Neustria and Burgundy (629–639). His capital was Paris. Dagobert II (d. 679) ruled Austrasia from 675. Dagobert III (d. 715) was king of the Franks (711–715), ruling over all three Frankish kingdoms, Neustria, Austrasia, and Burgundy.

Poitiers — none of the Dagoberts seem to have had any connection with Poitiers (<u>not</u> Poitiers-sur-Seine, of which I can find no trace), although Dagobert II does seem to have been placed in the custody of the Bishop of Poitiers in the 650s.

The Battle of Poitiers — (again <u>not</u> Poitiers-sur-Seine), also known as the Battle of Tours (732), is a signal event in French history, at which the Franks and Burgundians, under Charles Martel (688–741), defeated the invading Moorish forces from Andalusia, and killed the Umayyad leader, the Governor-General of al-Andalus. The three Dagoberts had all died long before the battle. In the *second* Battle of Poitiers (1356), which took place outside the city at Nouaillé during the Hundred Years' War, English forces under the Black Prince defeated the French army, and took captive the French king, his youngest son, and much of the surviving French nobility.

Goethe — Johann Wolfgang von Goethe (1749–1832), German poet, novelist, dramatist and all-round polymath.

Faites vos jeux — French for "Place your bets".

p. 36/37 GPU — predecessor of the NKVD and KGB, the Soviet-Russian secret police.

L'Intran — short form of *L'intransigeant* (The Intransigent), a newspaper that had run since the 1870s, and which had started as a leftist paper, but later moved to the far right and became fervently anti-Dreyfusard. Dreyfus, who was wrongly convicted of treason was of Alsatian origin, like Arp.

Citroën — Presumably refers to the automobile manufacturer.

List of Antoines / Antonys

Duchamp — French Dadaist and avant-garde painter.

Schoenberg — radical Austrian composer and inventor of the 12-tone system.

Matisse — French painter.

Picasso — Spanish painter, based in Paris. Known to Huidobro.

Picabia — French Cubist painter, whose father was Cuban. Friend of Huidobro.

Braque — French Cubist painter, and colleague of Picasso during the 1910s.

Stravinsky — innovative Russian composer, who created famous ballets for the Ballets Russes. The riotous première of his *Rite of Spring* in Paris in 1913 was one of the most famous musical events of the 20th century.

Brancusi — Romanian sculptor.

Mondrian — Dutch abstract painter.

Eluard — French surrealist poet.

Lipchitz — French Cubist and abstract sculptor. Friend of Huidobro.

Torres García — Uruguayan painter, active in Paris. A friend of Picasso.

Miró — Catalan painter/sculptor. Resident in Paris in the 1920s, he was a member of the Surrealist group with Arp.

Masson — French surrealist painter.

Aragon — French poet, and significant figure in literary Surrealism.

Varèse — French avant-garde composer, who later emigrated to the USA. A friend of Huidobro, he set some of the latter's work to music.

Ernest — this is most likely a typo for (Max) Ernst, the German painter and sculptor, who was a leading figure in the Dada movement and a close friend of Arp.

Vitrac — (Roger) Surrealist poet and playwright, who had previously been involved with the Dada group.

Léger — French Cubist painter.

Tzara — Romanian-French poet, and a leading figure in both Dada and Surrealism.

Gleizes — French Cubist artist, and author of the first treatise on Cubism.

Breton — French poet; leader of the Surrealist movement.

Klee — German painter; member of the Blue Rider group in Munich with Kandinsky (see below) and teacher at the Bauhaus.

Crevel — (René), French surrealist writer.

Hélion — (Jean), French abstract painter.

Gropius — German architect and founder of the Bauhaus.

Laurens — (Henri), French sculptor

Jolas — (Eugène), Alsatian-American writer, translator and critic; founder of the magazine, *transition*; promoter of James Joyce.

Giacometti — Swiss painter and sculptor.

Calder — American sculptor, best known for his mobiles.

Corbusier — Franco-Swiss modernist architect.

Dreier — (Katherine), American artist and collector.

Sima — properly (Josef) Šíma, a Czech abstract painter.

Daumal — (René), French surrealist writer.

Doesbourg — (here, Nelly); Dutch Dada artist; married to Theo, founder of the De Stijl movement and associate of Mondrian.

Taeuber — (Sophie), wife of Hans Arp; Swiss artist and designer.

Marcoussis — (Louis), Polish-French artist, involved with Cubism, and later designer and illustrator of surrealist books.

Kandinsky — Russian painter, leader of the Blue Rider Group in Munich, and teacher at the Bauhaus. One of the most significant abstract painters of the 20th century.

Chagall — Russian artist of Lithuanian Jewish background, born in Vitebsk, and later resident in France, where he took French nationality. While an avant-garde painter, his work was *sui generis*, and owed much to Jewish and Russian folk traditions.

Zervos — (Christian) Greek/French art historian (1889–1970) who had his own gallery in Paris and founded the influential *Cahiers d'Art* in 1926.

p. 38/39 *Mistinguette* — properly Mistinguett (Jeanne Florentine Bourgeois, 1875–1956), celebrated French actress and entertainer. Reputedly the highest-paid female entertainer in the world at one point, her legs were insured for 500,000 francs in 1919.

p. 40/41 *Storks* — the stork is almost a symbol of Alsace, and is the subject of many folktales.

polois(e) / Saintpolist — the word *polois* is almost certainly derived from the name Féraud de St.-Pol, author of the Alsatian nationalist "épisode lyrique", *Alsace et Lorrain* (1915).

Henner — Jean-Jacques Henner (1829–1905), Alsatian painter.

Yll / Ill — river that flows through Strasbourg.

Herman Chatriam / Erckmann-Chatrian — Huidobro has mis-transcribed the names here. Erckmann and Chatrian [sic] are the surnames of two 19th-century Alsatian writers who jointly authored patriotic novels and dramas.

coramine — stimulant for aiding respiration; a trade-name in the early part of the 20th C. Now known as Nikethamide or Nicotinic Acid Diethylamide.

mámaros / Mammarists — The Spanish implies "suck", "suckling" or "breast-feeding" but also, in Chilean Spanish, implies "rogue" or "cheat". Of course it also suggests "mammary", or breast (*mamário*), hence the translation used here.

Cayo Graco / Caius Gracchus — Roman Tribune of the 2nd century BC, and reforming politician, who was assassinated. Plutarch wrote a biography.

p. 42/43 *Moltke* — Helmuth von Moltke, the Elder (1848–1916). Head of the Prussian general staff and the architect of the defeat of both Austria and France by the Prussians – he was thus responsible for the fate of Alsace.

Coligny — Gaspard de Coligny (1519–1572), Admiral of France and Huguenot leader. Murdered in the run-up to the St Bartholomew's Day Massacre.

Isla de los cisnes / Isle of Swans — the Île aux Cygnes, an artificial island in the River Seine.

Hernán Cortés — conqueror of Mexico; with Pizarro, the most famous of the Spanish conquistadors.

p. 50/51 *neckties ... à la Duncan* — almost certainly refers to Isidora Duncan, a celebrated American dancer, who died of strangulation in 1927 when her neck-scarf became caught in the wheels of her open-topped car.

Tupungato — one of the highest peaks in the Andes, on the border between Chile and Argentina.

p. 52/3 *Galeries Lafayette* — famous department store in Paris.

p. 58/9 *Gilles de Raiz* — Huidobro's play was published in Paris in 1932, and excerpts were performed there the following year.

p. 62/3 *el marrano* — a *marrano* was a Jew forced to convert to Christianity during the Spanish Inquisition; as the choice of word appears to have been for its sound rather than anything else, the translation does not reflect this.

Pisco — grape-based liquor native to Peru and Chile.

p. 64 *Mari Aceituna* — literally "Mary Olive", this is a play on a phrase from Cervantes' *Novelas Ejemplares*: "en tiempos de Maricastaña, cuando hablaban las calabazas" (in the time of Maricastañā [Mary Chestnut] when pumpkins talked), meaning 'in days before recorded time'. I am grateful to the Argentine poet, Daniel Samoilovich for elucidating this.

p. 76/7 *Epaminondas* — 4thC BC Theban general who led Thebes to freedom from Sparta.

Pericles — 5thC BC Athenian orator, statesman and general during the Athenian golden age.

Achilles — legendary Greek hero at the Battle of Troy; one of the main characters in Homer's *Iliad*.

Aristides — Athenian statesman (530–468 BC) known as "The Just". A successful general in the Persian Wars.

Themistocles (524–459 BC) — Athenian politician and general during the early years of the Athenian democracy.

Alcibiades (450–404 BC) — Athenian orator, statesman and general, who fought on both sides during the Peloponnesian War, and, at one point, after making too many enemies in Greece, served in the Persian Empire as an adviser to one of the imperial satraps.

Battle of Lepanto — (1571), an important naval engagement in the Ionian Sea, in which the united Christian forces defeated the Ottoman fleet. Cervantes fought in the battle.

Tasso — Italian poet (1544–1595) famous for the epic poem *Gerusalemme Liberata* (The Liberation of Jerusalem, 1581), among others.

Charles V — (1500–1558), Duke of Burgundy (from 1506), King of Spain (from 1516), Archduke of Austria (from 1519), Holy Roman Emperor (from 1519).

Cerro Santa Lucia — Santa Lucia Hill is in the centre of Santiago.

Romulus and Remus — legendary founders of Rome.

p. 78/79 *El Greco* — Spanish painter of Greek origin (1541–1614). His name "The Greek" no doubt made it easier for those who found it too difficult to pronounce *Domenico Theotokopoulos*, his birth name.

p. 84/85 *Amieux Frères* — famous French brand of sardines. The translation uses *John West*, one of the most widespread British brands of tinned sardines.

San Isidro, labrador / St Isidore, the farmer (or *farm-worker*) — patron saint of Madrid.

p. 90/91 *Bouillon Kub / Maggi bouillon cube*: Bouillon Kub was the most common brand of powdered, cubed, vegetable stock, and known throughout Latin America in Huidobro's day. The translation uses a more modern international brand that might be recognisable to Anglo-American readers.

p. 92/93 *doña Pablo y Virginia / Lady Paul and Virginia* — probably drawn from the 18thC French novel, *Paul et Virginie*. Amongst the Spanish aristocracy, a combination of names such as this, using "y" (*and*) is not unusual, and reflects the patronymic and matronymic, in that order. The formula is not uncommon elsewhere in Spanish society; Picasso's surnames, for instance, were *Ruiz y Picasso*. Standard modern usage is to omit the *y*.

p. 94/95 *El Cid* — 11th century Castilian warrior, King of Valencia, and hero of the wars against the Moors; also the subject of Huidobro's novel, *Mío Cid Campeador* (1929; available in translation from Shearsman Books under the title *El Cid*). The Cid legend had it – and this was perpetuated in the 1963 Hollywood movie, starring Charlton Heston – that his corpse was strapped onto his horse and propped upright with his banner, and his appearance thus on the battlefield outside Valencia turned the tide of the conflict, the frightened Moors fleeing before the dead hero. Needless to say, this did not actually happen, but the legend was too good to ignore, both for the novelist *and* for the movie-makers.

www.ingramcontent.com/pod-product-compliance
Lightning Source LLC
Chambersburg PA
CBHW020029030726
47499CB00007B/2339

* 9 7 8 1 8 4 8 6 1 7 2 4 7 *